THE TWISTS AND TURNS OF LOVE

Barbara Cartland

Barbara Cartland Ebooks Ltd

This edition © 2022

Copyright Cartland Promotions 2022

ISBNs

9781788676625   EPUB

9781788676632   PAPERBACK

Book design by M-Y Books
m-ybooks.co.uk

THE BARBARA CARTLAND ETERNAL COLLECTION

The Barbara Cartland Eternal Collection is the unique opportunity to collect all five hundred of the timeless beautiful romantic novels written by the world's most celebrated and enduring romantic author.

Named the Eternal Collection because Barbara's inspiring stories of pure love, just the same as love itself, the books will be published on the internet at the rate of four titles per month until all five hundred are available.

The Eternal Collection, classic pure romance available worldwide for all time .

THE LATE DAME BARBARA CARTLAND

Barbara Cartland, who sadly died in May 2000 at the grand age of ninety eight, remains one of the world's most famous romantic novelists. With worldwide sales of over one billion, her outstanding 723 books have been translated into thirty six different languages, to be enjoyed by readers of romance globally.

Writing her first book 'Jigsaw' at the age of 21, Barbara became an immediate bestseller. Building upon this initial success, she wrote continuously throughout her life, producing bestsellers for an astonishing 76 years. In addition to Barbara Cartland's legion of fans in the UK and across Europe, her books have always been immensely popular in the USA. In 1976 she achieved the unprecedented feat of having books at numbers 1 & 2 in the prestigious B. Dalton Bookseller bestsellers list.

Although she is often referred to as the 'Queen of Romance', Barbara Cartland also wrote several historical biographies, six autobiographies and numerous theatrical plays as well as books on life, love, health and cookery. Becoming one of Britain's most popular media personalities and dressed in her trademark pink, Barbara spoke on radio and television about social and political issues, as well as making many public appearances.

In 1991 she became a Dame of the Order of the British Empire for her contribution to literature and her work for humanitarian and charitable causes.

Known for her glamour, style, and vitality Barbara Cartland became a legend in her own lifetime. Best remembered for her wonderful romantic novels and loved by millions of readers worldwide, her books remain treasured for their heroic heroes, plucky heroines and traditional values. But above all, it was Barbara Cartland's overriding belief in the positive power of love to help, heal and improve the quality of life for everyone that made her truly unique.

AUTHOR'S NOTE

Gambling losses and gains in the 1800s ran into astronomic figures among the Bucks in the London Clubs.

Charles James Fox, a compulsive gambler and Politian, would play for twenty-four hours at a sitting, losing five hundred pounds an hour.

To achieve more modern values we should multiply the sum by approximately twenty. In this story Sir Roderick would have won over one hundred thousand pounds.

The Royal Drawing Rooms that Queen Charlotte held every Thursday were altered to Evening Courts by King Edward VII.

I was presented at one in 1925 and one in 1928 after my marriage.

In 1939 after the outbreak of War, both Drawing Rooms and Levées were discontinued.

CHAPTER ONE
1802

The gentleman walking along down the rough gravel drive with its innumerable potholes slipped in his polished Hessians.

He swore under his breath and cursed himself again for having taken the wrong turning and landed up with a buckled wheel to his phaeton.

It was his own fault, he thought to himself, and he had no one else to blame.

He had left London very late after spending the night with a fair charmer, who was so entrancingly seductive that she made him forget the long journey that was waiting for him the following morning.

He had, however, driven very fast and his new team of chestnuts had indeed excelled themselves.

Even so it had meant that he had spent his first night much nearer London than he had intended, while on the second he had arrived later than was polite at the mansion of a friend where he had arranged to stay the night.

This meant that out of sheer courtesy it was just impossible for him to leave as soon as he had finished breakfast.

There had been horses to inspect and a number of gallant exchanges with his hostess and her plain daughters before finally he could be back on the road again.

He had been told of a short cut, which involved turning off the main highway, and now he knew that it had not only been a mistake but a disaster.

Driving at what he admitted was a dangerous speed along a narrow lane, at a blind corner he had encountered a farm wagon.

Only by the most skilful driving did he prevent a head-on crash between his horses and an aged farm animal.

Nevertheless the wheel of his phaeton had come into contact with that of the wagon and it was therefore impossible for him to proceed further.

The yokel had suggested that he might find help at The Manor House. So, leaving his groom in charge of his team, the gentleman, had passed through a pair of dilapidated gates to find himself in a drive that he felt could not have been repaired for at least a hundred years.

It was in fact extremely picturesque with the rhododendrons, lilacs and syringa bushes which bordered it all overgrown but a riot of blossom.

The gentleman, however, was concerned not with beauty, but in getting his fine phaeton back on the road.

He strode on as fast as he could along the drive, thinking that when it rained the resulting morass of mud and puddles would make it impassable.

Suddenly there was a turn in the drive and he found himself looking at The Manor House that he was seeking.

At first glance it was rather attractive.

Originally it must have been Tudor, but the creeper that grew all over it made it hard to distinguish its actual period.

There was a gravel sweep in front of the house, which was in the same state of disrepair as the drive and again there were a lot of shrubs, brilliant against what could be seen of the ancient weather-beaten bricks.

Looking quizzically at the house, the gentleman also noted that many of the top windows were apparently boarded up.

Even on the first and ground floors panes of glass were missing and had been replaced either with wood or cardboard.

The front door that was badly in need of a good coat of paint, was closed, but under the creeper growing around it, there was a bell-pull and a knocker that had once been brass but was now black and broken.

The gentleman tried both and waited.

Nothing happened and he thought it was more than likely that the occupants of the house were away from home.

He then decided that he would try the back door.

He walked round the house and saw, through an opening in an ancient red-brick wall, a kitchen garden where two people were working.

That, he thought, was more promising and he walked towards the nearer of them.

It was a woman wearing a faded cotton gown and a sun bonnet on her head.

She was planting seeds, bending over a long line marked in a small patch of ground that had recently been dug.

The gentleman next walked right up to her.

"I wish to speak," he said in an authoritative voice, "to the owner of the house, but I find it impossible to receive any answer at the front door."

At the sound of his voice the woman started and then straightened her back and he found himself looking at the face of a girl.

She was undoubtedly young and she was also exceedingly beautiful.

The eyes that looked enquiringly into his seemed to be unnaturally large in the shade of her sun-bonnet and were the deep blue of the periwinkles growing in profusion amongst the uncut grass beside the drive.

For a moment the girl seemed too surprised to speak, but when she did her voice was soft and cultured,

"I am sorry," she said. "The bell is broken so, if Annie was in the kitchen, she would not have heard the knocker."

Instinctively, as he realised that she was not what he had at first thought, the gentleman raised his hat.

"Am I speaking to the owner of the house?" he asked.

"You are," she replied simply.

"Then I have come to you for help." the gentleman said. "I have had an accident with my phaeton in a narrow lane about a quarter of a mile from your gates and I need a wheelwright."

"No one is hurt, I hope?" the girl asked quickly.

"No, it was not a bad accident," he replied, "but it prevents me from going any further and I am, as it so happens, in a hurry."

The girl who he was speaking to was, he now realised, looking at him with an undoubted expression of admiration on her face.

Belatedly he realised that he had been rather peremptory in voicing his request.

"My name," he then told her, "is Chester, Major Adrian Chester, and I am on my way to Kirkby Castle."

"My name is Petula Buckden," the girl replied, "and I expect you know already that this is Buckden Manor."

"I gathered that was the name of the village from the half-witted yokel who directed me here."

She glanced at him swiftly as if she was surprised at the tone of his voice.

"That, I imagine, will be Ned, if he was driving the wagon."

"He was," Major Chester admitted, "and, in case you are worrying, I can assure you that both Ned and the wagon are unscathed."

He spoke in a sarcastic tone that brought a flush of colour to Petula's cheeks.

She put down on the ground the seeds she was holding in a basin and walked towards an elderly man who was working further down the garden.

"Adam!" she called out. "This gentleman needs Ben to repair a wheel for him. Do you know where he will be?"

The man she was speaking to dug his spade into the ground and came towards her.

"You be askin' for Ben, Miss Petula?"

"Yes, Adam."

"'E'll be up with Farmer Jarvis if 'e ain't gone nowhere else.'

"Will you go and find him?" Petula asked. "Tell him that there has been an accident."

"It'll take me some time to walk to the farm, Miss Petula."

"Then you had better take the gig. Bessie has been out this morning, so take her slowly. She is getting too old for two journeys a day."

"I'll do that, miss."

Adam went back to collect his spade, moving at a rate that made the Major tap his foot impatiently and repress an inclination to assert once again that he was in a great hurry.

"It is doubtful if Ben could be here in under an hour," Petula said. "Perhaps you would like to bring your horses into the stables? If the wheel is badly bent, Ben will need to take it to his workshop."

"Where is that," Major Chester asked in the tone of one who expects to hear the worst.

"It is at the other end of the village."

"I might have guessed it!"

Petula laughed.

"I am afraid you will find in Buckden, as in most small places in Yorkshire, that what we do we do well, but it takes time."

The Major drew his watch from his waistcoat pocket.

"It is after three o'clock," he informed her. "How long do you think it will take me to get from here to Kirkby Castle?"

"I am afraid I have no idea," Petula answered, "Several hours at least."

She well knew that Kirkby Castle was the home of the Earl of Kirkby, who was the Lord Lieutenant of Yorkshire.

"It looks to me," the Major said, "as if I am going to be extremely late, if I arrive at all. Is there an inn nearby?"

"Not one where you can stay and certainly not one where you could stable your horses."

For a moment the Major looked at Petula almost angrily as if it was all her fault that the accommodation was so inadequate.

Then he smiled.

It transformed his face and, while before she had thought him a cold and autocratic type, she realised now that he also had charm.

She had in point of fact been overwhelmed by his appearance.

Never had she imagined that any gentleman could be quite so elegantly dressed and at the same time look so extremely masculine.

She realised that his white cravat was an intricate masterpiece and that the points of his collar, which reached slightly above his square chin, were the very latest fashion for a Beau.

She noted too how well his grey whip-cord fitted over his shoulders and, as he was still standing with his hat in his hand, she was sure that his hair was cut in the fashion that had been set by the Prince of Wales.

Because, however, she felt rather humbled by his magnificence and was well aware that in contrast she looked shabby and what she described in her own mind as 'a mess', she said shyly.

"If-you would like to fetch your horses, I will see that the stables are emptied of anything that has been stored there. We only have Bessie now and she is out in the fields at this time of the year."

"I would not want to put you to any trouble," the Major declared. "And I am hoping that, when the wheelwright can be found, my journey will not be long delayed."

Petula did not answer.

He thought that his hopes were unlikely to be realised and he must make the best of the situation infuriating though it was.

He therefore followed her as she walked to a building at the back of the house, which he realised was the stables.

They were in what the Major privately thought was a most disgraceful state of repair. Tiles were off the roof leaving great holes that undoubtedly let in the rain.

When Petula pulled open one of the doors, he saw that there had once been stabling for a dozen horses and the stalls were intact. However, they were dusty and dirty while the spiders had spun their webs from bar to bar.

"You are driving a pair, I suppose?" Petula asked him.

"No, four," Major Chester replied briefly.

Her eyes lit up.

"I have never travelled behind a four-in-hand," she said. "It must be exciting to move so fast."

"It is when one is travelling," the Major replied.

As he spoke, he realised that he was being ungracious, but he was still feeling angry not only at the delay but at being involved in an accident through his own fault.

He should not have left the main road and he should not have travelled so fast down a country lane. But what was the use of going over it all again.

He had better make the best of the situation and be thankful at any rate that there was a wheelwright within reach.

In the stables there were luckily four stalls that were not cluttered with old implements, packing cases and logs of wood.

"Adam will bring in some straw when he comes back," Petula said. "I am afraid your horses will not be very comfortable, but at least they can rest."

"You are extremely kind, Miss Buckden, and I am very grateful," the Major said.

"Perhaps before you fetch the horses I am sure that you would like some refreshment?" Petula suggested. "There is some cider in the house or tea if you prefer."

"I would find a glass of cider most acceptable," the Major responded politely.

Petula led the way round from the stables towards the front of the house.

Despite her shabby and faded cotton gown the man walking beside her realised that she moved with a lithe grace that he had not expected in a countrywoman.

His host's daughters of the previous evening had been thick-set and ungainly

In his mind he described them as being 'clumpy' and then found himself remembering the movements of the charmer who had made him late in starting on his journey.

'God deliver me from a woman whose feet are heavy as she crosses the floor,' he had thought.

Petula seemed to float rather than walk and, when she opened the front door and entered the cool low-ceilinged hall, she undid the ribbons of her sun bonnet.

She took it off as naturally as a man might remove his hat upon entering a house.

It was then that Major Chester told himself that she was indeed as unexpectedly lovely as finding an orchid growing on a rubbish heap.

Never before could he remember seeing hair that appeared like a great shaft of sunshine against the dark panelling of the hall and her complexion was pink and white like the almond blossom on the trees outside.

She carried her head proudly on a long neck that was as graceful as her movements and there was just a faint touch of amusement in her voice as she said,

"Perhaps you would not mind waiting in the drawing room while I go and fetch the cider for you? I am afraid that there is no one else in the house except my old Nanny, Annie."

"I don't wish to put you to any trouble, Miss Buckden," the Major replied.

"It is no trouble," Petula answered automatically.

She opened the door of the drawing room and he entered, looking abnormally tall and broad-shouldered, and then she ran down the long passage that led to the kitchens.

The house, which really needed at least a dozen servants to look after it, was hopelessly large for just herself and Annie.

They found that the only way they could manage was to shut up every room that was not needed and try to keep clean only the ones that were essential.

Petula found Annie, as she had expected, in the kitchen baking bread, which she did once a week.

"Your tea's not ready yet, Miss Petula," she said without looking up, "so it's no use you a-botherin' me for a crust from a hot loaf. I knows that's what you be after!"

"You are mistaken, Annie," Petula replied. "It is a flagon of cider I need."

"Cider?" Annie cried. "If Adam a-thinks he's havin' cider at this time in the afternoon, he's mistaken!"

"It is not for Adam," Petula said as she took a glass jug and a tumbler out of a cupboard. "We have a visitor."

"A visitor?" Annie exclaimed. "That be a change! Is it the Vicar?"

"No, Annie. It is the most magnificent gentleman you have ever seen. There has been an accident to the wheel of his phaeton and he ran into Ned's wagon."

"Then I'll bet that lazy Ned was asleep as usual!" Annie said sharply. "They've no right to let him drive when he's no idea which direction he's a-goin' in."

"The horse knows its own way home," Petula laughed, "and I have a shrewd suspicion, although I would dare not voice it to him, that the gentleman was travelling too fast."

"There's never been a gentleman as doesn't do that," Annie replied, "as I've said to your father often enough when he was alive."

"Papa seldom had good horseflesh to drive," Petula answered.

There was a little sob in her voice as she spoke and her eyes misted over.

It was hard now after nearly five months to think of her father without crying and it was still an agony to be without him.

She went into the cool larder that led off the kitchen. There was little enough nowadays to put on the wide marble slabs. She could remember that in her grandfather's day there were huge open bowls of cream, big pats of yellow butter and wicker baskets full of brown eggs.

Now there were only a few eggs from the hens that Annie treasured and were only eaten on special occasions and a jug of milk that Adam collected every morning from the adjacent farm.

There were under one of the slabs three large stone flagons of homemade cider, which were kept for occasional visitors and for Adam.

It was part of his wages, her father had always said and, although Annie sniffed and said that they could not afford it, Petula insisted that Adam was entitled to his daily glass of cider.

The flagons were refilled when they were empty and she tipped one cautiously, since it was very heavy, until she had filled the glass jug, which she had set down on the stone floor.

Carrying it back to the kitchen she put it on the silver salver that Annie had fetched from another cupboard and placed the tumbler beside it.

"It's a good thing I cleaned the silver two days ago," Annie remarked. "I kept puttin' it off until I was ashamed to look at it."

'I am sure our guest will be impressed at how well it shines," Petula commented.

Actually she felt that nothing in The Manor was likely to impress the Major favourably. At the same time it was rather exciting to have a visitor. Often weeks passed by and she saw no one except Annie and Adam.

Then she would make an excuse to go to the village simply because it was pleasant to chat with Mr. Yarrow, the butcher or Mrs. Blackburn at *The Crown and Feathers*.

It was only as she was walking back towards the drawing room that Petula thought of her own appearance and wondered if she should have gone upstairs and put on a better gown than the one she was wearing.

But she told herself it was unlikely that Major Chester would notice her at all and, if he did so, it would be in the condescending manner that he had spoken to her at first.

'He is obviously very puffed up with his own importance,' Petula thought. 'I expect he is wealthy. Rich men always seem to think that the world is theirs to walk on.'

She carried the cider into the drawing room and found that the Major was standing at the open window looking out over the uncut lawn.

The fields that bordered the garden sloped away towards a small wood beyond which there was undulating countryside rising in the far distance to bare topped hills.

"You have a most beautiful view from here, Miss Buckden," the Major said turning to Petula as she walked towards him.

"I love it," Petula answered, "but then I have not seen many other places."

"You have lived here all your life?"

"Yes indeed. There have been Buckdens in this house since the time of Queen Elizabeth, but they have never been great travellers."

The Major smiled as he poured himself out a glass of cider.

"I suppose by that remark you mean that you wish you could travel?"

"I would love to do so," Petula said, "and I am sure, now that the War is over, the people who have been confined to England during it are hurrying to go abroad."

"That is true," the Major agreed, "but those like myself who have had enough of fighting are content to stay at home."

"You fought against Napoleon Bonaparte?"

"For a short while," he replied, "but I was in India and took part in the wars there."

"How thrilling!"

There was no doubt that Petula was interested.

"I would love to hear about India. All the East sounds so fascinating. But perhaps that is only because I know so little about it."

"Parts of India are, as you say, fascinating," the Major said, "but it is also very hot and war can be extremely uncomfortable."

He spoke in a dry voice, which made Petula feel as if he had no wish to discuss it with her.

They therefore lapsed into silence until the Major put down his tumbler and said.

"Thank you. The cider was very pleasant. Now, as you suggested, I had better fetch my horses and put them into your stable until the wheelwright tells me how long he will take to repair the phaeton."

"I am afraid that it will take Adam quite some time to reach the farm where we think he is working," Petula said apologetically.

She looked at the clock and then she added,

"As I think it – unlikely that your wheel will be repaired before – dinnertime, would you like something to eat before you proceed on your way?"

She spoke a little hesitantly because she was wondering almost wildly what they could offer him.

The Major also hesitated.

"I feel that I have already put you to a great deal of inconvenience, Miss Buckden," he said. "Perhaps your local inn will provide some sort of a meal for myself and my groom."

"It will only be bread and cheese. I am sure Annie could do better than that, although naturally it will not be the sort of fare that you are accustomed to."

"As a soldier, I can assure you that I have not always been well-fed," the Major said with a smile, "and I shall be very grateful indeed, Miss Buckden, if I could avail myself of your hospitality before I set off on what will undoubtedly be a long and tiring drive."

"Then we will do our best," Petula promised simply, "but please don't be too critical."

"I promise you I shall only be extremely grateful for your kindness," he answered.

Petula waited until he had left the house and was starting to walk back down the drive before she ran to the kitchen.

"Quick, Annie, quick," she cried, "he is staying here for dinner and his groom will also want something to eat."

"Staying for dinner? Whatever are you talkin' about, Miss Petula?"

"Major Chester. He has gone to fetch his horses to put them in the stables and Adam has driven to Jarvis's to find

Ben. He will be hours about it, as you know, Ben will never hurry himself."

"You're expectin' me to provide dinner. Miss Petula? With what, I ask you?"

Petula made a little gesture of helplessness.

"There must be something in the house, Annie."

"There's a wee bit of lamb I was savin' for your luncheon tomorrow, Miss Petula, and there's a few eggs, but nothin' else that I can recall."

Petula had gone to the larder door to look almost despairingly at the empty slabs.

Then she gave a cry.

"There is a rabbit on the floor, Annie. Adam told me he had caught it in a snare and was taking it home for his dog."

"Well, that be better than nothin'!" Annie exclaimed and added. "His dog indeed! He'll eat it himself, the greedy pig, and us half-starvin'!"

"Adam works hard and he has to eat too."

"Not our rabbits," Annie said harshly.

"If there is any over, you will have to give him some," Petula said soothingly. "After all, it was his snare and if the rabbits belong to anyone they belong to him. We cannot claim what we cannot catch or shoot."

"I'm not arguin' about it. Miss Petula," Annie said. "If Adam did as he was told, there'd be a lot more to eat in this house than there is."

"At this time of the year – " Petula began to say.

Then she knew it was no use arguing with Annie. Although she was country born and bred, she still persisted in believing that birds were plentiful all the year round and there was no breeding season to interfere with her larder of pigeons, partridges and hares,

Petula gave her the rabbit and Annie then set it down on the table, It was a young one but large enough to provide a meal unless the diner in question was very hungry.

"Here are the eggs so that you can make an omelette, Annie," Petula proposed,

"Usin' all my eggs!" Annie exclaimed in a note of horror. "Those were supposed to last you and me, Miss Petula, for several days."

"I will look for nests you have not found," Petula promised, "and now I am going into the garden to find what vegetables we have."

As she reached the door, she turned to say,

"Thank goodness there are a few ripe strawberries on the South wall, which will do for dessert. I know you have some cream hidden away."

"All I can say is that you and me, Miss Petula, will both be goin' hungry for the rest of the week," Annie complained.

"We will manage somehow," Petula smiled and ran off to the garden.

There was so much else to do that she felt she had hardly time to breathe before she saw Major Chester returning down the drive.

He was leading two horses and his groom behind him was leading another two and the sight of them made Petula forget everything else.

Never in her life had she seen such magnificent animals or a team so perfectly matched.

With their long manes and tails and with their chestnut coats seeming to shine in the sun, they looked, Petula thought, as if they had just stepped from a painting by George Stubbs.

The Major led the way towards the stables and she followed them noting that his groom wore an exceedingly smart Livery with a crest on his silver buttons.

"I believe there is straw for them somewhere, Jason," the Major said, "but the man who was to provide it for us has gone in search of the wheelwright."

Before the groom could reply in what Petula was sure would be a supercilious manner, she interrupted.

"It is stacked in the last stall and I will help you spread it."

"Certainly not," the Major called out sharply. "Jason will do that if you will show him where it is."

She knew that he was not only replying to her, but was also giving an order to his groom.

She therefore walked on to the far end of the stables where the straw that was to make a comfortable bed for Bessie during the winter had been thrown down by the boy from the farm who had brought it to them.

"It is here," Petula told him.

The groom looked at it and to her surprise replied in a very pleasant tone,

"Thank you, miss. Leave it to me. The horses won't want much as we won't be stayin' long, but they could do with a drink."

"The pump is outside in the yard."

"Thank you, miss."

She thought that the groom seemed more amenable than his Master. Then, because she felt a little in awe of the Major, she asked tentatively.

"Was there – any sign of Ben when you – fetched your horses?"

"I thought, as you had already warned me that in this part of the country you make haste slowly, it would be a mistake to be too optimistic."

"He cannot be very much longer," Petula said.

Major Chester did not answer and she went on,

"Perhaps you would like to come to the house and rest? Dinner cannot be ready before another hour or so."

"I have no intention of walking any further," the Major said, "and so I suppose your man will know where to take the wheelwright."

"There is only one road into the village," Petula answered, "so it would be impossible for him to miss a phaeton, a vehicle we do not often see in these parts."

She was not being sarcastic, but she felt that her visitor was being a little high-handed. Although she told herself it was childish, she rather resented his sneers at their slowness.

"Go back to the phaeton, Jason," the Major said to his groom, "and fetch my valise. Then find out where this man, Ben, is taking the wheel and impress on him the need for speed. Will there be a moon tonight?"

"No, not this week," Petula said before the groom could reply, "and I think you will find it difficult even with the lanterns on your phaeton – to find the way to Kirkby Castle."

"It will be light until about ten o'clock," the Major said almost as if he spoke to himself.

Petula realised that he was calculating how soon the wheel was likely to be mended and, once it was, how far they would have to travel to the nearest Posting inn.

"There is one at Huntingford," she said as if he had asked her the question. "It is about three or four miles after you get back onto the main road."

She saw the Major's lips tighten and after a moment in a nervous little voice she said.

"If it proves – impossible for you to – get away tonight, we will then – try to make you comfortable here."

"You are very kind, Miss Ruckden," the Major said, "but I am sure that it will be quite unnecessary for me to impose upon you any further."

Petula felt as if he had deliberately snubbed her.

She next walked out of the stable and back towards the house.

She had reached the front door before the Major caught up with her.

"You must forgive me," he said, "if I sounded somewhat abrupt and was not as profuse in my thanks for your offer of hospitality as I should have been. Quite frankly I had not until that moment envisaged that I might not be able to get away tonight, but I do see now it may well be impossible."

He spoke with a warmth in his voice and a sincerity that had not been there before.

"I – quite understand," she replied shyly. "I cannot offer you very much, but at least — it is a roof over your head."

"I have a feeling," the Major said, "that I am behaving rather badly like a spoilt child."

Petula laughed.

"Perhaps we all do so when we are disappointed. Was there an exciting party waiting for your at Kirkby Castle?"

"I hope not," the Major said fervently. "There is nothing more tiring than a large dinner party with a crowd of strangers after you have just driven a great distance."

Petula, who had never been to a large dinner party, thought it would in fact be a thrilling event however tiring the journey might be, but aloud she said,

"Instead you will have neither a large party nor a large dinner, but, as Annie has said ever since I was a child, 'what cannot be cured must be endured'."

It was the Major's turn to laugh.

"I can remember my old Nanny saying exactly the same."

"Mama told me that they all have a language of their own."

They reached the hall and she added,

"I thought you might like to wash after driving so far and I have put some warm water and towels in one of the bedrooms."

"You think of everything, Miss Buckden," the Major smiled.

She went up the stairs wondering as she did so if she had indeed remembered everything.

There had been the table to lay for dinner, there had been the bedroom windows to open, water to be heated and taken upstairs and a dozen other things that Annie asked for and could not cope with herself.

The room she had prepared for the Major was her father's and had so not been shut up like most of the other bedrooms on that floor.

She showed the Major into it and felt that, although the carpet was very shabby and the curtains faded, it was a very pleasant room with its four-poster bed in which generation after generation of Buckdens had been born in and slept and died in.

"I hope you will find all – you need," Petula said nervously.

She was wondering if she should offer him her father's hairbrushes.

He must have guessed what she was thinking because he said,

"My man is bringing me my valise from the phaeton so I shall be self-sufficient."

Only as Petula hurried down the passage to her own room did she wonder if the Major would have liked a bath.

But Annie could not have both heated the water and cooked the dinner she told herself.

She reached her own room and, as she glanced in the mirror, she then realised that she looked extremely untidy.

Her hair wanted brushing and was curling in riotous tendrils around her cheeks.

Her gown that was one of her older ones that she wore only to work in the garden was creased and stained with earth from when she had been planting seeds.

'He must think I am an absolute hooligan!' Petula exclaimed.

Pulling off her clothes, she washed in cold water and then went to her wardrobe.

There were not many gowns for her to choose from, because since her mother's death and her father's illnesses, they had been so poor that she had never been able to afford a new one.

She could not afford to go into mourning and had gone on wearing her ordinary clothes except that she added a black sash and black ribbons to her bonnet when she went to Church on Sundays.

Then she remembered that in a cupboard in her bedroom were all her mother's clothes.

She had always intended to use them as she longed to put on anything that belonged to her mother.

'What can I wear?' she asked herself, but there had been no occasion until now to wear anything but her own threadbare dresses.

Annie, if no one else, would have thought it extremely ridiculous for her to be dressed up when there was no one to see her and no one to entertain.

Now Petula felt that she had an excuse for looking like, as Annie would say, 'a proper young lady'.

She opened the cupboard door where her mother's gowns were kept and there was the fragrance of roses.

It was the scent that her mother had always distilled herself and wore, so that whenever the roses came into bloom, it was an unforgettable reminder of her.

For one moment Petula closed her eyes and felt the pain of loss within her breasts, which was always there when she thought of her mother and knew how much she missed her.

She took down a gown, which was a pale blue with a white fichu round the shoulders and which had been the fashion five years earlier.

It had a full skirt, but then Petula did not realise that these were no longer worn. To her it looked beautiful and luxurious.

She laid it out on the bed and started to arrange her hair in what she imagined would be a fashionable style.

This was difficult because the only guide she had to what was being worn in the world outside Buckden was an occasional copy of *The Ladies Journal* that came her way.

Fortunately her naturally curly hair looked attractive whatever she did to it and, when she put on her gown, Petula knew that she looked smarter than she had ever been before.

She only hoped that the Major would appreciate the effort she was making on his behalf, but thought it unlikely.

There was no time to linger. She had taken far longer to dress than she had intended and, with just one last look in the mirror, Petula hurried down to the kitchen.

"Have you everything you need, Annie?" she asked.

"I can manage, Miss Petula," Annie replied, "though I'm well aware it's not a large meal for a gentleman as is used to at least half-a-dozen courses."

"Do you think he really eats half-a-dozen every night?" Petula asked curiously. "He is very slim and surely, if he devoured as much as that, he would be fat."

"Half-a-dozen be a small dinner in a gentleman's house," Annie pointed out firmly.

She was an authority, Petula knew, because before she had come to work for her mother, Annie had been nursery maid in a Nobleman's household in another part of the County.

It had been an enormous house and ever since she had been tiny Petula had been regaled with stories of how things were done properly by the 'gentlefolk'.

"I've no time to talk now," Annie said sharply. "I suppose you didn't think to offer the gentleman a glass of wine?"

"Wine?" Petula asked in surprise. "But we have none."

"There's three bottles of your father's claret in the cellar that I've been hoardin' against an emergency," Annie answered. "I've brought a bottle up, opened it and it should be the right temperature by now."

"Oh, Annie, how splendid of you. I had no idea that we had any wine hidden away."

"I wasn't lettin' just anyone have it, or that Adam who's always got his tongue hangin' out for a drop of liquor," Annie replied. "But I a-took a peep at our visitor as he walks back from the stables and he's a gentleman if ever I've seen one."

"Yes, he is," Petula agreed, "and I am glad we have some wine to offer him, Annie."

"There's lemonade for you, Miss Petula, and I've got out extra glasses you'd forgotten."

She pointed with a floury finger to the sideboard.

"How was I to know there was anything to fill them?" Petula asked. "Thank you, Annie, you are a marvel."

She thought as she carried the glasses from the kitchen into the dining room that this was just the sort of situation that Annie enjoyed.

She was a really excellent cook as her mother had trained her well and her father had an appreciation of good food that made it a challenge to live with him.

If Annie cooked anything that he greatly enjoyed, he never forgot to thank her, but she was also fully aware when her dishes went wrong and Sir Martin found them unpalatable.

Petula knew that, although the food they would have tonight would be simple, it would be very edible and she would be surprised if Major Chester, however grand he might appear, did not enjoy it.

Of one thing she was certain, that he would be feeling hungry and her father had always said that was a better reason for eating than any other he knew.

It seemed almost like old times to have a man in the house.

As she now moved towards the drawing room, she felt that what she missed more than anything else was her father's voice calling her as soon as she came into the house.

She opened the drawing room door.

Her guest was seated in an armchair and, as she stood for a moment looking at him, he rose to his feet with a smile on his lips.

'This is going to be a most exciting evening,' Petula told herself, 'and something I shall remember for years to come.'

CHAPTER TWO

As Petula stared at him, she realised that the Major had changed into his evening clothes.

If she had thought that he had looked smart before, it was now impossible not to gasp at the elegance of his blue long-tailed coat and skin-tight pantaloons that the Prince of Wales had brought into fashion for informal occasions.

A fob glittered from his waist, but otherwise he wore no jewellery and so the elegance of his skilfully tied snow-white cravat needed no embellishment.

As if the Major realised that she was surprised at his appearance, he said.

"I must after all accept your kind offer of hospitality for the night, Miss Buckden. The wheelwright informs me that it is impossible for him to complete the work that is required until tomorrow morning."

Petula was unable to find her voice and he went on,

"I hope that neither I nor Jason will be too much of a trouble to you. He is not only my groom but can valet me in emergencies such as this and assist your Nanny in the kitchen,"

"There is no – need for that," Petula murmured.

She felt as if the Major had taken over the house and it was now under his command.

She walked across the room conscious that her mother's gown gave her confidence and feeling that, although she was not too sure of it, there was just a touch of admiration in the Major's eyes.

He was in fact as stunned by her appearance as she had been by his.

If she had looked very lovely, as she certainly had in her faded gown with her hair untidy from working in the garden, she was now, he thought, breathtakingly beautiful.

His experienced eye noted that her gown was old-fashioned, but then it became her and the white muslin that framed her shoulders revealed the perfection of her skin.

Her hair was becomingly if not skilfully dressed and seemed almost like a golden halo to frame her large eyes and heart-shaped face.

'She is so lovely and would be a sensation at St James's,' the Major said to himself.

Then he thought cynically that country flowers did not transplant and it would be such a pity to spoil what was perfect in its own environment.

"I hope you have found everything you – require," Petula was saying a little breathlessly.

"Jason, like myself, is an old campaigner," the Major replied with a smile, "and, what he thinks I need, he commandeers in a quite ruthless fashion."

Petula now felt that she should sit down and suggest that her guest did likewise, but at that moment the door opened and Jason announced,

"Dinner is served, ma'am!"

Petula gave a little laugh.

"It all sounds very grand and I hope you will not be disappointed."

"Shall I say I am starting to find this a very interesting not to say exciting adventure?" the Major said. "And infinitely preferable to the large and doubtless dreary dinner party you envisaged for me."

"It might have been very entertaining," Petula replied as they walked towards the door.

"That is what I think our evening here will be," the Major answered.

She felt herself blushing as there was a note in his voice that she had not heard before.

She had arranged the dining room table with care, choosing the lace-edged tablecloth that her mother had always kept for best and setting on it the four silver candlesticks that had been in the Buckdens' possession since the reign of King George I.

In the centre of them she had set a low bowl filled with syringa and pink rhododendrons and she had also brought out her mother's best china, which had hardly been used since her death.

She thought with satisfaction that she need not be ashamed of the setting for their dinner and she was sure that Annie would not let her down when it came to the meal.

It was only when she seated herself at the table that she had gone instinctively to her usual chair and had left the head of the table to the Major.

He made no comment but seated himself as if by right in the chair her father had always used.

Then, as Jason carried in the first dish, Petula saw that Annie was determined to show their guest that she knew how gentry ought to behave.

There was soup to start with from the stockpot that Annie always kept simmering on the stove to which had been added, Petula guessed, the mutton bone and parts of the rabbit that would not be produced later.

It was indeed stunningly delicious and the Major, offered the tureen for the second time, finished everything that was left.

After that there was a spinach soufflé that had been one of her father's favourites.

Petula had found just enough young spinach in the garden for what she thought would be a vegetable for the main course.

"This is exceptional," the Major exclaimed. "You are fortunate, Miss Buckden, that your Nanny is such a good cook."

"Mama taught her when she first came to us," Petula replied, "and Papa was always very particular about what we ate."

The Major made no further comment, but he ate every piece of the rabbit, which Annie had made with a fine sauce to which Petula was sure had been added some of the claret that he was drinking without comment.

The few small strawberries she had picked from the South wall of the garden were only enough for one person.

So as not to make the Major feel at all embarrassed at eating alone, she remarked lightly that she did not care for strawberries and was looking forward to the plum season.

He certainly showed no sign of embarrassment when Annie's newly cooked loaf, hot and crisp from the oven, was set in front of him with a cream cheese and a large pat of butter.

He cut himself a large slice saying,

"I realise gratefully how extremely fortunate I am in not having to put up at *The Crown and Feathers*."

Jason, who had waited on them silently and with an expertise that Petula felt must come from long practice, set the decanter of claret on the table and withdrew.

The Major filled his glass, then sat back in his armchair very much at his ease and Petula thought with an air almost as if he owned the place.

"Now," he proposed, "let us talk about ourselves."

They had conversed throughout dinner about horses, the need for the roads of London to be repaired, the vast acres of uncultivated land in Yorkshire and various impersonal subjects.

To Petula it had all been very interesting because she had never before dined alone with any man except for her father.

"I am afraid there is little for me to tell you about myself," she answered, "but I would like to talk about you."

"That, as it happens, is not a subject that interests me at the moment," the Major replied. "I suppose there is no need for me to tell you that you are extremely beautiful."

Petula looked at him in astonishment.

Not only had no one ever told her anything of the sort, but she felt that it was a surprising statement from the Major.

He had seemed so condescending when he had first arrived and had up to this moment made her feel as if nothing was really good enough for him.

She felt the colour rise in her cheeks. At the same time she knew that he was waiting for her answer.

"There is – really no one here," she said in a hesitating little voice, "to – notice what I look like. Adam only admires the vegetables in what he calls 'his garden'."

She gave a little laugh and continued,

"And the Vicar is – half-blind. He does not even see when the choirboys are behaving badly in Church."

"And what is your future to be?" the Major next enquired.

Petula made a little gesture with her hands.

He noticed how graceful they were. Her fingers were long and slim and, despite the fact that she gardened, well kept.

"I cannot – answer that question," she replied. "I have been expecting to hear from my uncle, but, although I have written to him twice, I have received no reply."

"You think he will decide what shall happen to you?"

"I really – don't know," Petula answered. "I have not seen him for many years – but he is my nearest relative."

"You can hardly live here alone for ever," the Major remarked.

Petula thought that he was thinking of the dilapidated house, the holes in the roof of the stable and the overgrown garden.

Some pride she did not know she possessed made her lift her chin a little higher.

"This is my home," she stressed quietly, "and I love it."

"And you are quite content to stay here whilst hiding your light under a bushel?" the Major asked. "Then let me tell you again it is a very lovely light."

"I think you are – flattering me," Petula said uncomfortably. .

"I am merely telling you the truth."

"I would like to believe you," she answered, "but even if I did, it would not alter my future, which as far as I am concerned, is a complete mystery."

"You are beginning to intrigue me."

The Major poured himself another glass of wine and asked her,

"What man would not be intrigued? And think what a story it would make."

He sipped the claret reflectively before he went on,

"I break down in a country lane, find a crumbling old Manor House half in ruins, but in it is someone so beautiful, so unusually lovely, that she could, if she so wished, take London by storm!"

For a moment Petula listened to him spellbound and then she laughed.

"Your story ought to have a happy ending with a Fairy Godmother waving her wand and transplanting the heroine to London. Alas, that is something – that will never happen to me."

"Can you be sure of that?" the Major enquired.

"*If wishes were horses, beggars could ride*," Petula flashed, "but I feel that in London beggar maids do not arouse much attention."

She had an unselfconsciousness which the Major felt he had never found in any other girl of her age, not that he had conversed with many young women and certainly had never dined with one alone.

"Tell me what you think about when you are alone here," he questioned.

He saw a twinkle in Petula's blue eyes as she replied,

"I spend a lot of my time thinking over what we shall have to eat. As you saw when you arrived, I have usually to work for my dinner."

'It is doubtless more arduous than singing for it," the Major said, "but, when you are not working, what interests you then?"

"Reading and thank goodness there are a great number of books in the house."

She smiled as she went on,

"I am sure that you would find them very out of date because they were bought by my grandfather, but to me they contain the world which I cannot travel in and the people I shall never have the chance of meeting."

"Suppose we look at your books?" the Major suggested.

"Would you really like to see them? I would not like you to sneer at them, at any rate not in their hearing."

"I promise you I will not sneer," he said, "and I will be extremely polite as I always am, as it happens, towards knowledge of any sort."

"Then do come with me," Petula proposed simply.

He opened the door and she preceded him from the dining room along a passage.

The paint had peeled from the walls and the pictures there were dark with age.

The furniture had been dusted, but there were handles missing from the chests, chairs had broken legs and wicker seats had not been repaired.

The Major noticed everything, while to her it was too familiar to arouse any comment:

She passed the door into the drawing room where they had sat before dinner and opened a door at the far and of the passage.

It had been, the Major saw at a glance at one time a magnificent library with shelves reaching from the floor to the ceiling, many of them filled with books, but others had large gaps that he felt must once have held leather-bound volumes.

Petula followed the direction of his eyes and said,

"A dealer bought quite a lot of the best books when Papa was ill. He would not give me much for them and I miss them sadly, but they provided the few necessities that the Doctor claimed that Papa must have."

She was not, the Major knew, seeking sympathy from him but merely stating a fact.

He looked at the books that were left and realised that there was a large variety of a type that would interest a scholar more than a young girl.

"Do you in truth find these books really interesting?" he queried.

"Absorbingly so," she answered. "Especially history and poetry."

The Major did not speak and she carried on,

"I cannot tell you how grateful I am to Grandpapa for having a literary taste. Papa and, as far as I can make out, most of my ancestors only cared for horses."

"I thought you liked mine," the Major commented,

"I know they are superlative," Petula answered, "but I hardly dare to look at them in case they leave me with no affection for poor old Bessie, who has served us well and faithfully for years."

"Once again you are making yourself out to be a beggar maid," the Major said. "But let me tell you that your face is your fortune and with so much wealth I refuse to feel sorry for you."

Petula looked at him mischievously.

"I wonder how much it would fetch in a sale room?" she asked. "Or do you think that a usurer would advance me a good price for it?"

The Major was just about to make the kind of witty rather risqué reply that would have been thought extremely amusing in London, but he then checked himself.

He knew that Petula spoke to him in all innocence and again without a touch of self-consciousness.

As if she thought that his attention had wandered from the books, she suggested,

"Shall we go into the drawing room? I think Annie will have made some coffee for you, but I am afraid I cannot offer you a glass of port."

"I am most content with the excellent claret I have enjoyed at dinner," the Major said. "I was expecting perhaps another glass of cider."

"That was all I thought I should be able to offer you for dinner," Petula explained, "but Annie always hoards things away against a rainy day and you are undoubtedly a tempest!"

The Major laughed and they walked back into the drawing room.

As she expected, there was a tray on which stood a small silver teapot that her mother had always used and two cups and saucers, which actually were all that remained of a set that had been broken one by one over the years.

Petula poured out a cup of coffee for the Major and then asked,

"Will you excuse me if I go and speak to Annie and see that she has made up the bed for you?"

"Jason will have already told her that we are staying," the Major replied.

"I think I will speak to her too," Petula insisted.

She went from the drawing room leaving him alone and ran upstairs to the room that he had used before dinner.

Annie was there drawing the curtains and turning back the bed, which had already been made up with the best linen sheets.

"The dinner was just perfection, Annie," Petula cried, "And the Major ate everything and you really are a genius."

"You'd have to be a real magician to feed a hungry man in this house," Annie replied uncompromisingly.

At the same time Petula sensed that she was pleased at the praise.

"You had something to give his groom?"

"He's had your dinner and mine for tomorrow and, if you go hungry, don't blame me!"

"I will not," Petula answered her, "and it is very exciting to have a visitor."

Annie made a noncommittal sound and then she said,

"I'll be movin' my things for the night into the room next to yours, Miss Petula. I only hope the mattress is not as damp as I expects it to be."

"Moving into the room next to mine?" Petula asked in astonishment, "but why?"

"I knows what's right," Annie replied. "and I'll be a-waitin' up for you, Miss Petula, to make sure you lock your door before you go to bed."

"Lock my door?" Petula repeated. "I cannot think what you are talking about."

"Then it's time you learnt that young ladies of your age, Miss Petula, are chaperoned," Annie snapped, "and, as your poor mother, God rest her soul, can't act in that capacity, I must do my best."

Petula laughed.

"Oh, Annie, you are quite ridiculous. If you are frightened of what people will say about the Major staying here tonight, who's to know except Ben and Adam?"

Annie did not answer and Petula kissed her on the cheek.

"You are an old fusspot!" she scolded, "but you are also a wizard cook, I was so proud of you when each dish was more delicious than the last."

She left the room as she finished speaking knowing that it was impossible to resist the urge to return to the sitting room and be with the Major.

'I may never again have a chance to talk to such a magnificent man,' she told herself. 'I must not miss a minute of it.'

He rose as she came back into the drawing room, then seated himself in a chair that had its back to the window so that Petula sat opposite him with the evening light on her face.

The sun was setting slowly and the shadows like the hills in the distance were purple and mysterious.

Through the open windows came the shrill high cry of the bats and the deep caws of the rooks going to roost. Otherwise there was a stillness that seemed to have something magical about it.

These were the sounds that Petula heard every night and her eyes were on the Major's.

She saw that his were grey, steely grey, and she thought there was something penetrating about them as if he looked deeply into her mind seeking for something although she had no idea what it was.

Because she felt a little shy, she said impulsively,

"Annie has made everything ready for you and – you will think it very funny – she is so afraid of the gossips that she has moved into the room next door to mine and has told me I must lock the door."

She waited for the Major to laugh, but, when he did not, she went on.

"I asked her who was likely to talk about my being unchaperoned except for Ben who is only interested in wheels and Adam who only wants to talk about potatoes."

"I am glad you are well looked after," the Major remarked.

"I told Annie that she is an old fusspot," Petula remarked, "but she was delighted that you enjoyed your dinner."

She paused before she asked a little anxiously,

"You *did* enjoy it?"

"More than I can tell you," the Major answered, "not only because the food was so good but because I had such an exceptionally interesting companion."

For a moment Petula could not think who he meant and then she smiled and said,

"Now you are being flattering again. Tell me all about the lovely ladies you dine with in London. They must be very amusing to be with. What do they talk about?"

"Themselves and, of course, love," the Major responded.

"Love?" Petula questioned, "but – "

Her voice died away and after a moment the Major asked.

"But what?"

"I was just going to say that you could not want to talk about love with everybody whom you dine with. Or perhaps you only dine with one special person who you do love?"

The Major smiled secretly at the innocence of the question, but aloud he said,

"If you think of love in the abstract, it is an absorbing subject to most people."

"I never thought of it as – being like – that," Petula stammered.

"What did you think?"

"I thought that you met somebody," she replied slowly, "and, when you – got to know them well, you realised that you wanted to be with them for the rest of your life and they felt the same."

"After that, what do you expect to happen?"

She hesitated and could not look at him so that her eyelashes were dark on her cheeks.

"I suppose – " she said in a hesitating little voice, "they kiss each other."

"And one should only do that when one was really in love?" the Major asked.

"Of course," Petula replied. "One could not kiss just anyone – otherwise – it would be – horrid!"

Again the Major smiled to himself.

"And you think that one day it will happen to you? But if you live here and see no one except Ben and Adam, where will your Prince Charming come from?"

"I cannot imagine, although I am very sure, if Fate decrees and the Gods are propitious, he will appear," Petula replied lightly. "Perhaps he will have an accident – with his phaeton in the village!"

She spoke teasingly and the Major knew that she was not being coquettish or flirtatious as any other woman might have been.

"That is always a possibility," he replied. "Or he may drop down the chimney like Father Christmas!"

Petula's laughter rang out.

"He would most certainly not look very attractive covered in soot! Besides our chimneys being so old and twisted he would have to be an acrobat to get down them."

"That might well prove to be an obstacle to true love," the Major replied dryly.

"But it would make an exciting story," Petula said. "Oh dear, you are making me feel that there are a great many deficiencies after all in my grandfather's library."

"Shall I suggest instead that you come to London in search of adventure and, of course, the Prince of your dreams?"

For a moment Petula did not answer, but looked out of the window at the darkening sky.

"I sometimes tell myself a story," she eventually answered, "that I go to London and I do in fact find someone I love, get married and live happily ever after."

She spoke in a dreamy voice and then her lips curved again in a spontaneous smile.

"Then I remember that I cannot afford the stagecoach, even to the next town, let alone London. And it would be a very very long walk."

The Major laughed.

"I am afraid that you are a pessimist. Most girls of your age, and certainly those who are beautiful, would not be waiting for Fate to suddenly occur or for an accident to happen in the village. They would fight by hook or by crook to get what they wanted."

Not realising what she was doing Petula rose to her feet and walked towards the window.

"You are making me feel that I am foolish and unenterprising," she said. "In fact I am not quite – certain what I do want."

The Major had followed her and now stood a little behind her as he said.

"Surely you want what every woman wants? Love and a man to look after you?"

She did not answer and he continued, his voice deepening,

"As I have told you, Petula, you are very beautiful and there would be a great number of men who would only be too willing to lay their hearts at your feet."

"If I have to go looking for them, it would then spoil the romance. In the storybooks the Knight kills the dragon and saves the damsel in distress. She does not go hunting for him."

That, the Major thought suddenly, was exactly what was wrong with the women he knew in London.

They were all too ready to do their own hunting. In point of fact they had usually laid out the dragon one way or another long before the Knight appeared.

He was about to speak, but Petula went on,

"I am thinking about what you have said. I shall remember this conversation after you have gone, but I do not feel I have the – courage to do the sort of things you suggest and I am quite sure that Mama would not wish me to go to London – alone."

"I was not really envisaging you doing so," the Major retorted.

"Then that makes it very simple," she replied. "And I shall have to wait until I am asked and, if nobody asks me, I must just – stay here."

She looked at him with the animated expression of a child who has just worked out a rather complicated sum.

Then, as her eyes met his and it was impossible to look away, she felt as if something very strange and inexplicable vibrated between them.

Everything else seemed to fade away except the Major's eyes and there was something magical that linked them like a shaft of moonlight.

How long they remained spellbound Petula could never calculate, but quite suddenly and unexpectedly the Major said almost harshly,

"I have had a long day and, as I must be up early tomorrow morning, I think I would be wise retire."

For a moment Petula could not find her voice.

Then vaguely, as if she had just come back to earth from the height of a mountain, she replied,

"Yes, yes – of course – Annie will have put a candle in the hall to – light you up the – stairs."

She would have moved away from the window, but the Major was standing just behind her and it was impossible for her to step back into the room until he did so first.

Once again his eyes were on her face.

"When you are older, Petula," he declared in a deep voice, "you will realise that I am behaving as your mother and Annie would wish me to do."

Petula looked at him enquiringly and he knew that she did not understand him.

He took her hand in his.

"Goodnight," he said, "and thank you not only for your hospitality but also for showing me that there are still things in this world that are unspoilt and just as lovely and pure as God intended them to be."

He kissed her hand and she felt his lips against her skin hard, warm and at the same time strangely compelling.

Then he turned without a word and he was gone from the drawing room, closing the door behind him.

She stood where he had left her, conscious only that at his touch something very strange had happened to her body.

It was a feeling that she could not understand. She only knew that it left her breathless and tongue-tied and at the same moment vibrating as if to music.

She stood still for what might have been a second or an hour. Then, as if she remembered her duties, she closed the window, latched it and drew the curtains.

She moved sure-footedly over the darkened room and without the need of a candle went up the stairs and into her bedroom.

She could hear Annie moving about in the next room and she had just undressed when she opened the door to say,

"Lock your door, Miss Petula, and no arguments about it!"

"Yes, of course, Annie, if you want me to."

It was always easier to do what Annie wished than to try to force her own way.

Annie closed the door and Petula knew that she was waiting outside.

She turned the key loudly in the lock and only then did she hear Annie go to her room.

Petula climbed into bed, but she could not sleep.

All she could think about was the feeling of the Major's lips against the back of her hand and after a while she put it on the pillow and laid her cheek against it.

She felt as if it gave her again that strange, unaccountable sensation that seemed to linger in her throat now.

'He will be gone tomorrow,' she told herself, 'but I shall remember for ever everything he said to me and how he looked.'

She must have fallen asleep at some stage in the night for she awoke to find that Annie was in the room pulling back the curtains.

"I had to wake you early, Miss Petula," she said. "With two men in the house and those dratted hens not having laid a single egg!"

Petula sat up in bed to see that Annie was dressed,

"I will go and fetch some from the farm," she said.

"That's what I thought you'd say," Annie answered, 'I'd have sent Adam, but he hasn't arrived yet. And he's so slow it'll be luncheontime before he brings me what I want."

"It will not take me more than ten minutes across the fields," Petula asserted.

She jumped out of bed as she spoke, washed and dressed herself. She was about to put on one of her own faded gowns when she hesitated and turned once again to the cupboard that contained her mother's things.

Last night the Major had thought her beautiful, but perhaps this morning he would see that he was mistaken.

Searching in the cupboard she chose a very pretty gown that her mother had worn only once or twice.

Annie would think it strange, Petula thought, that she should put it on to walk the fields, but she was quite sure that she would not have time to change when she returned before the Major came down to breakfast.

It was still very early, the sun had not properly risen and was only a glow in the East.

The dew was on the grass as Petula hurried across the fields holding a wicker basket on her arm.

The Home Farm where they obtained their milk had once served no one but The Manor House and the other farms on the estate.

The only money that Petula had to live on was the rent paid by the tenant farmers.

These rents were very small because the farm houses and buildings were in such a bad state of repair.

Mrs. Holbridge the farmer's wife was a fat and pleasant woman and she greeted Petula warmly.

"What can I do for you, Miss Buckden?" she asked. "You're surprisingly early."

"We had a guest last night," Petula answered, "a gentleman had an accident in the lane and Ben is mending his wheel."

'Then he'll want sommat fillin' for his breakfast," Mrs. Holbridge smiled.

"I would be very grateful if we could have some more eggs. Annie used them all up for dinner last night."

"A hungry man'll want more than an egg for his breakfast," Mrs. Holbridge replied. "I'll give you a cut off our home-cured bacon."

"That would be very kind of you, Mrs. Holbridge, and, of course, I will pay you back."

"You'll do nothin' of the sort, Miss Buckden," Mrs. Holbridge replied. "But don't you go tellin' Mr. Holbridge or he'll deduct what I'll be givin' you off the rent when he pays it. There's none more close-fisted than a Yorkshireman!"

She laughed at her own joke and Petula looked with satisfaction at the large number of brown eggs she was putting into her basket, the slices of bacon and several cuts of ham.

"I wish we still had a farm of our own," she said impulsively.

Mrs. Holbridge followed her train of thought.

"Aye, we lives well," she said, "but we works ever so hard for it. The men were down in the field afore light this morn."

"My father always said what a good farmer Mr. Hobbridge was," Petula said politely,

"Your father were a real gentleman, miss, and I be sure you miss him."

"I do," Petula answered.

She felt that Mrs. Holbridge might be about to embark on a long and rambling anecdote about her father that she had heard before, so she quickly took up her basket.

"Thank you, Mrs. Holbridge. You are an angel and I am very very grateful," she said and started back towards The Manor before there could be any further delay.

It had taken her longer than she had expected to reach the farm as the grass had grown higher in the last few weeks and it impeded her progress, especially as she was wearing her mother's full-skirted gown.

So she walked along the side of a field where she could move quicker even though it was a longer way round to The Manor.

It also meant that, unless she was to climb a hedge, she must pass through the edge of a small wood before emerging directly below the lawn.

It was cool and shadowy under the boughs of the birch trees and the blue-bells, which had made a carpet as blue, were now fading a little.

But there were still primroses vividly yellow in the moss and some white violets, which, Petula told herself, she must pick as soon as she had time.

There was a little path winding between the trunks of the trees and she was just reaching the end of it when she saw with a leap of her heart someone coming towards her.

There was no mistaking it was the Major and she saw that his polished Hessians were dusty with pollen.

She drew nearer to him and knew that her heart was beating in a most peculiar way and, although she wanted to call out to him, the words would not come to her lips.

"Annie told me where I would find you," he began, as they met face to face. "As I was hungry for my breakfast I thought I might help you to carry it."

"Thank you," Petula smiled, "but it is not – really very – heavy."

She wondered why her voice sounded so strange and then once again, as she looked up at the Major, it was impossible to look away.

"I also wanted to say 'goodbye' to you," he said, "which is something I omitted to do last night."

Petula thought that his voice was rather odd. But she could think of nothing except for his eyes looking deep into her heart.

The Major took the basket from her arm and set it down on the ground and then, while she waited, feeling as if she was in a dream, he put his arms around her.

"I could not sleep for thinking about you," he said and his lips were suddenly on hers.

For a moment Petula could only feel surprise that this should be happening.

Then the sensations that she had felt in her body when he had kissed her hand were there again, only intensified until she felt the wonder of them invade her like a streak of sunlight.

The Major's lips were at first hard against the softness and innocence of hers, then they were tender and gentle so that she felt as if her whole being reached out to become a part of him.

It was so wonderful and so perfect that Petula felt as if they were alone in a secret place far removed from the world, a place of magic and indescribable beauty, and a glory that was part of God.

The Major held her captive and she thought that her soul passed into his keeping before he said in a voice that was curiously unsteady,

"That is the right ending to a Fairy story."

Petula could not move, she could only look up at him, her eyes filling her whole face and telling him without words what she felt.

She thought that he would kiss her again, but he then said abruptly,

"We must go back. I have to be on my way as soon as possible."

CHAPTER THREE

The phaeton disappeared out of sight at the turn of the drive and Petula stood for a long time looking at the place where she had last seen it.

Then a sigh seemed to come from the very depths of her being.

This, as the Major had said, was the end of the dream.

They had walked back to the house in silence, until, as they stood on the unkempt lawn, he turned to look at her face with an expression in his eyes that she could not fathom.

"This has been a dream," he said quietly, "an enchantment that I think neither of us will ever forget."

He paused for a moment and then added,

"We will not meet again, Petula, but never will I find elsewhere such a perfect moment of magic."

He had not touched her, but she felt from the deep note in his voice that he still held her in his arms.

As if he forced himself, he walked on and into the house through the open window of the drawing room.

She knew that he did not want her to follow him and Petula had taken her basket round to the kitchen entrance.

Annie was fussing and fuming in the kitchen.

"How could you have been so long?" she asked. "The gentleman is up and wantin' to be on his way."

Petula did not reply. She only went up to her own room to stare at her face in the mirror as if she felt that it must have completely changed.

She could still feel the impression of the Major's lips on hers, still feel that his heart was beating against her breasts as he held her close against him.

It was as if she walked in a dream, but the dream was coming to an end when she would awake to find reality.

She was aware at the back of her mind, although somehow she could not bring herself to think clearly, that the Major was having his breakfast and that Jason had brought the phaeton round to the front door.

Then at the very last minute when the Major was picking up his high-crowned hat in the hall, she had walked down the stairs.

Knowing instinctively that she was there, he raised his eyes to watch her coming slowly down with the grace that he had noticed the first time they had walked from the garden to the house.

She held her chin high, but her eyes were large and dark in her small face.

When she reached the hall, she stood looking up at the Major and it seemed as if again they were both spellbound.

"Goodbye, Petula," he said and his voice, although very low, seemed to vibrate round the small hall.

"Goodbye – " she replied and the word was hardly above a whisper.

For a long long moment they looked into each other's eyes.

Then one of the horses waiting outside the door shook his bridle and broke the spell.

Without another word, without touching Petula's hand, the Major walked down the steps and climbed into his phaeton.

Hardly aware that her feet were actually moving, Petula followed to stand watching the horses going away, noting with one part of her mind the expert way that the Major handled them.

Jason raised his hat, but the Major looked ahead, his lips set in a tight line, his chin very square.

The phaeton lurched over the potholes in the drive, but it was only a question of seconds before the horses, fresh and eager to be on their way, had reached the turn.

Then they were out of sight.

'I shall never see him again,' Petula murmured beneath her breath.

She waited for the pain to strike her almost as if she drove a dagger into her own breast.

Still feeling as if she was not yet really awake she walked across the hall as Annie came hurrying down the passage from the kitchen.

"Miss Petula, what do you think?" she cried.

Not waiting for Petula to answer she went on,

"That gentleman's groom pressed somethin' into my hand when he says his 'goodbye' and told me that he and his Master had spent a most comfortable night. Most grateful they were for the hospitality we gave them."

She opened her hand as she spoke and stared at what if contained before she carried on,

"I didn't look at what he'd given me until now, but see what it is, Miss Petula!"

With an effort Petula forced herself to look at what Annie held in her hand.

There were two large gold coins, each one she knew worth five guineas!

"Ten guineas, Miss Petula," Annie said in awestruck tones. "Ten guineas for one night. I can hardly believe what I sees with me own eyes."

"You – you gave them a very g-good dinner," Petula said in a voice that did not sound like her own.

"Well, we'll certainly not go hungry this week," Annie exclaimed. "I told you he was a real gentleman and there's no mistake about that."

"No, Annie, there is no mistake about that," Petula agreed and walked into the drawing room.

There were a dozen things that she ought to be doing and she was sure that Adam was expecting her in the garden.

But all she could think of was the elegance of the Major when they had talked here and the feelings she had when she had stood at the window with him just behind her.

Now she knew, although she had not realised it at the time, that she had wanted him to kiss her and he must have felt the same.

She knew now that was what he had meant when he had said,

"When you are older, Petula, you will realise that I am behaving just as your mother and Annie would wish me to do."

If he had only kissed her then, she now thought, she would have not only one enchanted moment to remember but two.

'I must go back to the wood,' she told herself.

She wanted to hold onto the wonder and glory that had happened there before she lost it as she had lost the Major.

She walked through the window and onto the lawn, but she had not gone more than a few yards when she heard Annie's voice.

"Where are you a-goin', Miss Petula? I wants you to help me make up the bed."

Petula turned round.

Annie was speaking to her from the window of the room that had been her father's and where the Major had spent the night.

"Can it not wait?" she asked.

"I want to do it now before I goes to the village," Annie replied.

Reluctantly Petula retraced her steps into the house and walked up the stairs.

Annie had already stripped the linen sheets from the big four-poster and was opening out another pair that she had taken from the linen cupboard.

"Come along, Miss Petula," she said sharply. "It's unlike you to be dawdlin' about the place. I was thinkin' we could have a nice bit of beef for luncheon. We can certainly afford it this week."

She threw a sheet across the bed and Petula automatically began to open it.

It smelt of lavender because her mother had always insisted that fresh bags of lavender be made every year for the linen cupboard at the same time that she made *pot pourri*.

"I don't know why we are making up this bed again," Petula remarked. "The Major will – not be coming – back."

There was a little throb in her voice as she spoke the last words, but Annie did not notice.

"I've a feelin' in my bones," she answered, "that having had one visitor we might have another."

"That is most unlikely," Petula replied, thinking that there would not be another accident in the village for perhaps twenty years.

"Have you forgotten we're still expectin' your uncle?"

"He did not answer my first letter, so there is no reason to expect that he will reply to my second."

"One never knows," Annie commented. "Postmen are none too reliable and we're a long way away from London."

Then, as they covered the top sheet with the blankets, Annie said in a different voice.

"I was just thinkin', Miss Petula, that it'd be unwise for you to tell anybody, especially your uncle, if he ever does arrive, that the gentleman stayed here last night."

Petula looked at her and Annie went on,

"You know just as well as I do that people have nasty minds and even longer tongues. I looked after you as your mother would have wished, but who would believe the word of a servant?"

She spoke without bitterness and continued,

"Now you be a sensible girl and do as I say. Just forget that we had a visitor, though it's grateful enough we are for what he has left behind."

As if she suddenly realised that Petula was unresponsive, she added,

"Promise me, dearie. I know what's best and you can trust me to decide what's right."

"I do trust you, Annie," Petula replied, "and, of course, I will promise, if it will make you happy."

"That's my girl," Annie smiled approvingly.

She picked up the velvet cover and she and Petula spread it over the bed.

"I'll brush the floor and then draw the curtains again when I comes back," Annie said, "and now I'll get my bonnet and cape. Luncheon'll be a wee bit late, but it'll be well worth waitin' for."

She bustled away down the passage and Petula stood for a moment thinking that this was where the Major had slept last night.

His head had touched the pillows and he had seen himself reflected in the walnut-framed mirror that stood over the inlaid chest of drawers that her father had always used as a dressing table.

She went to the window.

Across the field she could see the spring green of the trees in the wood.

As if afraid that she would once again be stopped, she ran down the stairs, out through the drawing room window and across the lawn as swiftly as her feet could carry her.

*

Luncheon was not finished until two o'clock, but Annie had enjoyed the beef she had brought back from the village and the excellent cheese that they completed the meal with.

It had, however, been difficult for Petula to force herself to eat anything.

She felt as if every mouthful stuck in her throat and it was an effort to swallow it.

But she knew how disappointed Annie would be, so she forced herself to look as though she was eating all her helping.

When Annie left the room to fetch something from the kitchen. she placed the slices of beef on her plate back onto the dish beside the joint hoping that Annie would not notice.

"Let's hope," Annie said as she cleared away, "you'll put on a little weight in the next week or so. I'm sick and tired of takin' in your gowns round the waist and the best present you could give me would be the need to let them out again."

"I am no thinner than Mama was," Petula answered. "Her gown last night fitted me very well."

"Your dear mother was nothin' but skin and bone for the last years of her life," Annie answered, "waitin' hand

and foot on you father, worryin' about him and you. She was like a sylph, as I always says to her."

Petula smiled,

"You would very much like me to be as plump as a German *Frau*, Annie, and that I have no intention of ever being."

As she spoke, she opened the dining room door to carry the plates into the kitchen.

Even when they were alone Annie would never allow Petula to eat anywhere but in the dining room.

"I knows what's right Miss Petula," she said. "I'm not havin' you sittin' down in my kitchen, which isn't your rightful place, as you're well aware."

It made a lot of extra work and a lot of walking about, Petula thought to herself.

But she realised that Annie was trying hard to preserve some semblance of gentlefolk's behaviour despite the fact that they lived in a house that was crumbling about their ears and possessed hardly enough money to keep themselves alive.

As she reached the passage, she stopped.

"What is it?" Annie asked who was just behind her.

"I think it is someone at the front door."

Petula put the plates she was carrying down on a table in the passage and walked towards the hall.

The door had been left open after the Major had departed and now to her astonishment she saw through the open doorway a vehicle standing outside.

For one moment her heart missed a beat as she thought that the Major had returned. Then she realised that it was not a phaeton she saw but a post-chaise drawn by two horses.

Already in the hall and standing some way from the door, so that she had not noticed him at first, was a gentleman.

She glanced at him and realised, although she had not seen him for ten years, that it was her uncle.

There was indeed a strong resemblance to her father, but Roderick Buckden, slenderer and dressed in the height of fashion, was far more elegant than her father had ever managed to be.

"You must be Petula," he exclaimed.

"Uncle Roderick – you have come at last," Petula cried. "I thought that you could not have received my letters."

I received a letter from you three weeks ago," he replied, "when you referred to one you had written earlier. That one never reached me."

"I sent it to the only address that Papa had for you," Petula exclaimed. "Then, as you did not reply, I thought I should write again and remembered that your Club was St James's."

"It is indeed one of my Clubs," her uncle answered. "But you must have written to an old address. That is the explanation why I did not come at once and I had no idea that your father was dead."

"He died just before Christmas."

"I am so sorry. I should have been here for the funeral."

Her uncle spoke rather vaguely and Petula realised that he was looking round the hall at the panes of glass that were missing in the long windows either side of the front door, at the paper peeling from the walls above the pictures and at the stair-carpet that was so threadbare that it was hard to know what colour it had been originally.

"The place looks much shabbier than I remember it," he remarked.

"I am – afraid so, Uncle Roderick," Petula replied, "but then there has been no money to spend on repairs or redecoration and Papa was very ill before he – died. I suggested writing to tell you so, but he did not wish to be a trouble to anyone."

Her uncle's face seemed to soften a little. She thought he had a hard expression and his eyes were certainly disapproving at what they saw although she could not blame him for that.

"I presume," he said, "that what you are implying is that there is little of value left in the house?"

"I have sold only a – few things," Petula admitted apologetically, "to provide Papa with medicines that the Doctor ordered and the food – he claimed was essential."

"So, I am the Beggar Baronet!"

"You have naturally inherited the title, as Papa had no – son."

Her uncle then looked at her face for the first time.

"Well, he certainly has a very pretty daughter. You had best tell me what else is left, but first I must pay the post chaise."

As he spoke, his driver, a surly-looking man in an ill-fitting coat, carried in two valises which he set down just inside the front door.

"'Ere they be, Gov'nor," he said, "and, if you've no further use for me services, I'll be on me way."

Petula saw her uncle draw a sovereign from his pocket.

The driver took them, stared at them disdainfully and said,

"That don't leave me much for meself."

"You have had what is your due," Sir Roderick replied, "and those last horses were not worth hiring."

"You're lucky to find an animal with four legs in this benighted part of the world," the driver retorted acidly.

He put the sovereign in his pocket and walked away without raising his cap.

"Impertinent fellow!" Sir Roderick remarked to Petula, "but at least I have managed to get here, although damned expensive it has proved to be."

"I am sorry, Uncle Roderick," Petula said as if he accused her of it being her fault.

"The house appears to be in a rotten state," Sir Roderick commented walking towards the drawing room.

"The top floor is uninhabitable," Petula answered. "And Annie and I have shut the rooms we are not using, but I am afraid a number of the ceilings have fallen in."

Sir Roderick looked all round the drawing room as if he was appraising everything in it and was disgusted with what he saw.

He sat down in a chair.

"Have you had luncheon?" Petula asked him politely.

"Yes, I called at a Posting inn two hours ago," her uncle replied, "but I would like a drink if there is anything left in the cellar."

"There are, I believe, two bottles of Papa's claret," Petula answered.

She remembered as she spoke how the Major had enjoyed it last night.

"Well, that is better than nothing," Sir Roderick condescended.

"Shall I fetch it for you?" Petula enquired.

'In a moment. Let me look at you. I thought when I was last here, was it nine or ten years ago, you were a pretty little thing. Now, dammit, you have grown into a real beauty!"

"I am glad you approve of me, Uncle Roderick," Petula, said, "because you are my only relative – left."

"I suppose that is true," he agreed reflectively. "But what about your mother's side of the family?"

"You know that Mama's family lived in the North of Scotland and most of them I think are dead. Anyway they gave up writing to her a long time ago."

"Then there is only you and I to represent the Buckdens," Sir Roderick said, "but it does not appear as if we have much to represent!"

"Are you going to live here, Uncle Roderick?"

"Live here," he exclaimed. "Good God, no! What I am wondering is if there is any fool likely to buy it from me."

Petula could not have been more surprised if he had exploded a bomb under her feet.

"But, but – Uncle Roderick," she then expostulated, "it has been in the family for three hundred years!"

"Who cares if it is three thousand?" her uncle replied. "What I want, Petula, is not this dilapidated ruin in the middle of nowhere but some money."

"That is something we certainly do not have."

"How many acres?" he enquired.

"Just over seven hundred. The three farms are let, but they pay us very little rent because the houses and outbuildings are in such bad repair."

Her uncle's lips tightened and she went on tentatively,

"There was a man here about six months ago – just before Papa – died who asked me if the house was for – sale."

"Who was he? Did you get his name?"

"Yes, he was a man called 'Barrowick' and I think he is very rich. He has a factory about thirty miles away and Annie thought that he had pretensions of being 'Lord of the Manor'."

"Pretensions is the right word," her uncle replied. "You say he is rich?"

"That is what Annie was told in the village, but I only spoke to him for a few minutes."

"And you told him that the house was not for sale?"

"Of course," Petula answered, "I had no idea that you would ever think of – disposing of what has always been an – heirloom handed down from – father to son."

"Well, I certainly cannot afford an heir," her uncle said, "so the sooner this encumbrance is off my hands the better!'

"B-but – Uncle Roderick – " Petula began.

Then she thought that anything she might say would be a waste of her breath.

She could understand in a way what her uncle felt.

At the same time it seemed wrong that he should be so anxious to be rid of The Manor, even though she knew that it would cost hundreds, if not thousands of pounds, to restore it to its original state.

Her uncle had risen from the chair to walk to the window.

"Seven hundred acres," he said reflectively, "the house and I suppose that there are a few cottages?"

"Twelve," Petula said automatically.

Her uncle did not speak, but she knew that, looking out at the fields, he was calculating exactly what he could obtain from Mr. Barrowick if he was still an interested purchaser.

She drew in her breath.

"If you – sell The Manor, Uncle Roderick," she asked in a nervous little voice, "what is to become of me?"

Her uncle did not answer for a moment.

Then he said,

"Come here, Petula."

Obediently she went to his side and he half-turned from the window to look at her.

The sun on her face revealed the clearness of her skin, the vivid blue of her eyes and turned her hair to shining gold.

"I have an idea," he began slowly.

"An idea, Uncle Roderick?"

"No, dammit!" he exclaimed. "It is more than an idea. It is an inspiration!"

"What is?"

His eyes left her face and she knew that he was looking at her figure, appraising her, she thought, almost as if she was a well-endowed horse.

"Do you know what I am, Petula ?" he then asked.

"What you are, Uncle Roderick? I don't understand."

"Then let me tell you. I am a gambler. So it is my fellow men and the Social world that amuse me, not because I am obsessed as so many rakes are by the turn of a card, but simply because I have to live."

"But – what happens if you – lose?" Petula asked.

Her uncle smiled.

"Then I am in the uncomfortable position I find myself in at this moment of owing more than I possess."

"You mean – you are in debt?"

"Exactly."

"So that is why you will have to sell The Manor."

"There is no alternative. At the same time, although that may solve my problems for the moment, there still remains a question mark over the future."

"You mean you may easily be in the same – position again once all the – money has run out?"

"Very easily."

Petula waited, but she was beginning to feel afraid.

It did not seem as if her uncle would give her and Annie anything to live on, in which case what would become of them?

"I told you I was a gambler," her uncle said slowly, "and, when one gambles, Petula, one develops an instinctive sense."

"I don't – understand," she said quickly. "Please explain it to me."

"It is difficult to put into words," her uncle replied, "but sometimes I know before the turn of a card what it will be and sometimes a feeling I cannot explain saves me at the very last moment from disaster."

He spoke in a strange tone, almost Petula thought, as if he was seeing clairvoyantly what might happen and then he declared,

"Now I have this feeling about you."

"A-about me, Uncle Roderick?"

"I know that *you* are the right card for me to play at this precise moment."

Petula waited.

She did not like to say again that she did not understand.

"What we are going to do," Sir Roderick said, "is to return to London as Sir Roderick Buckden with his beautiful niece who is a great Yorkshire heiress."

Petula stared at her uncle as if she thought that he had taken leave of his senses.

"An – heiress?" she repeated, thinking that she could not have heard him aright.

"An heiress!" he repeated firmly. "Beauty is important in the world I live in, Petula, but not as important as money."

"B-but – but we have no – money."

"We shall have what I will get from the sale of the estate."

"You know it will not be much."

"Yes, I know that and you know that," Sir Roderick said, "but nobody else will know it."

"I still don't – understand."

"Let me put it very clearly. You, my most attractive niece, are going to find yourself a rich husband. As soon as you are married, you will pay me half of everything your husband gives you. And with your looks it ought to be a very considerable sum."

Petula was speechless. She could only stare at him.

"So you can leave the Marriage Settlement and all other financial problems to me," Sir Roderick said airily. "All you have to do is to captivate one of the rich men I shall introduce you to and you can believe me when I tell you that I know a great many."

"Why – should they wish to – marry me?"

Sir Roderick smiled as if the question was so childish that it was hardly worth a reply and then he said,

"A beautiful woman, young and unspoilt, is quite a rarity in London at this moment, but beauty is very considerably enhanced by a golden halo. That, my dear, is what everyone will believe you have."

"But – it is – untrue!"

"As I have already said, nobody else will know that."

"But – Uncle Roderick, I do not think I am in any way – capable of – acting such a – lie of pretending that I am – rich when I have – nothing."

Petula spoke hesitantly and was conscious that her uncle's eyes narrowed.

"Of course, if you can keep yourself adequately without my assistance, you can always refuse my offer."

"You know I – cannot do – that," Petula whispered.

"Then stop arguing and leave everything to me," her uncle said. "Go and fetch that bottle of claret you were talking about and then I would like to see the estate accounts, if you keep them."

"Yes, I keep them," Petula answered him.

She went from the room to fetch the bottle of claret that Annie had hidden away.

When she then brought it back into the drawing room a little later, she felt as if her mind could not take in what her uncle had just said to her.

It seemed really impossible that he should mean her to act a part that she felt she was fundamentally unsuited to and which would be a lie intended to deceive someone who would obviously trust her.

'I cannot do such a thing,' Petula told herself, 'Papa would not approve of it and Mama would be – horrified.'

But, she asked herself, what was the alternative?

She was increasingly afraid of the answer even as it formed in her mind.

After some difficulty in finding a vehicle to convey him to Huntry where Mr. Barrowick had his factory, Sir Roderick left The Manor at about ten o'clock the following morning.

He had no sooner driven away than Petula ran into her father's library and took out his will from a drawer in the desk.

Her uncle had asked for it last night and she had told him she had mislaid it, but would find it by the time he returned.

"I don't suppose it is worth the paper it is written on," he blustered, "but I might as well see it."

"I think, Uncle Roderick, Papa thought that – you would look – after me."

"And that is exactly what I intend to do," her uncle insisted.

He talked to Petula until late in the evening and everything he said made her feel more and more afraid of her future.

What had horrified her more than anything else was when she asked a little tentatively, because she almost anticipated the answer.

"Will I be able to bring – Annie with me to London?"

"Certainly not!" her uncle had responded. "To begin with I cannot afford it and secondly your lady's maid must be well trained in the arranging of your hair in a fashionable manner and is used to looking after expensive gowns."

"What – will happen to A-Annie?" Petula asked him almost piteously, "Papa would have given her a pension."

"What with?" her uncle asked almost brutally.

After they had retired to bed, Petula had lain awake, not thinking about herself but about Annie.

How could she possibly abandon her old Nanny penniless and at her age unlikely to find other employment?

Then, just as her uncle had had an inspiration, she had one too.

Now she drew out her father's will and added a codicil to it.

It was not difficult to copy her father's handwriting and Petula inscribed on the heavy parchment,

"*To Annie Bacon, who has been in my employment for so many years, I leave for her lifetime Honeysuckle Cottage and to Adam Ives also for his lifetime No. 1, Church Cottage, both on my estate in the village of Buckden.*"

Petula then signed her father's name at the bottom of the codicil, copying it exactly from the signature above it. Then, carrying the will in her hand, she went into the kitchen.

"I have only just realised, Annie," she now said, "that, when you witnessed Papa's will, you omitted to add your signature to the codicil. For it to be legal you should have signed it twice."

"Surely it is too late now?" Annie asked.

"Of course it is not," Petula answered. "You were there when Papa signed his will and you verified his signature."

"Yes, of course," Annie agreed.

Petula put a pen in her hand.

"Sign, here, Annie," she asserted.

The old maid obeyed her, scrawling her name rather laboriously.

The other witness to her father's signature had been the Doctor. But then he, however, had left the village soon after her father's death to take up a more lucrative post in Richmond.

His signature was a little difficult to copy, but Petula managed it.

Then she left the Will on the desk ready for her uncle's return and hurried back to the kitchen.

"Now listen to me, Annie," she said, "this is important and you can stop whatever you are doing."

"I suppose you want some luncheon," Annie retorted.

"That is quite immaterial compared with what we have to do now."

Petula spoke in a voice that made Annie look at her in some surprise.

"My uncle is taking me with him to London," she said, "but he is making no provision either for you or for Adam."

She saw Annie's cheeks pale and so she added quickly.

"But my Papa remembered you. He left you Honeysuckle Cottage, Annie, which as you know is empty at the moment since old Mrs. Burton died three months ago."

"Honeysuckle Cottage," Annie quavered. "Well, that was real kind of your father, Miss Petula, but I never thinks as I'd be leavin' you."

"I don't wish to leave you, Annie, but I have to do what Uncle Roderick wishes."

"I understand," Annie said, but Petula sensed that she was upset.

"We will talk about that later," she said quickly. "What we have to do at this moment is to furnish Honeysuckle Cottage."

"Furnish it? What do you mean, Miss Petula?"

"Uncle Roderick has gone to Huntry to sell the estate to that man who called when Papa was ill. He intends to sell everything, as he put it, 'lock, stock and barrel'."

"Then what are you sayin', Miss Petula?"

"I am saying that you are going to have the things that are really mine, the furniture that belonged to Mama and all the little things she loved and I love too because they belonged to her."

"What will your uncle say?"

"He will not know," Petula answered. "He has not even bothered since he arrived to go round the house. How could he be aware of what is in my bedroom where we put so many of Mama's treasures or what is left in the other rooms?"

She saw that Annie understood what she was saying and turned towards the door.

"I am sending Adam to the farm to borrow Ned and the wagon and you and I will get what we can down into the hall."

Afterwards Petula thought that only by being so authoritative and, as Annie said, 'taking her breath away from her', was she able to get her own way.

Fortunately they both knew Honeysuckle Cottage well and as it happened it was about the only cottage on the estate that was not in a very bad state of repair.

Old Mrs. Burton, who had died there, had been a widow with a certain amount of money of her own,

She had therefore not relied on Sir Martin to repair and redecorate the small cottage she rented from him, but had paid for the work herself.

She had even added on to the original cottage which meant that there were now two bedrooms, a pleasant sitting room and a small dining room opening out of the kitchen.

All day until it was dark Petula and Annie carried things down the stairs and filled up the wagon with the help of Adam and Ned.

Then sitting in the front of it they drove to Honeysuckle Cottage and arranged everything in the small rooms.

Petula insisted on taking the best carpets, the rugs that were not too worn and choosing the prettiest and least faded curtains for the windows.

"I can't be a-takin' all this, Miss Petula," Annie muttered a dozen times.

"Do you wish Mr. Barrowick to have it all?" Petula would ask angrily. "And what will he do with it? Put it on a bonfire, I should not wonder."

Annie was silenced and they went on working.

They were both exhausted by the time they went to bed, but Petula was up again at five-thirty driving Annie to bring down more things.

There were mirrors from her mother's bedroom that she felt were of no great value, but she had known them since she was a child.

There was linen from the cupboard on the stairs and she found a small disused canteen of silver that was not marked with the Buckden Crest and which she insisted on Annie having.

"You are taking them for me as well as yourself," she repeated to every protest the old woman made.

By noon Honeysuckle Cottage seemed crammed from floor to ceiling.

Petula then told Adam that his cottage was his for life and that he was to take every tool he was likely to require to work his own garden and perhaps to go out jobbing in the village.

Adam did not argue.

He filled his wheelbarrow with forks, spades, hoes, trowels and watering cans to trundle them down the long twisting path through the shrubberies, which was the quickest way to his small cottage which stood next to the churchyard.

When Petula came back to The Manor, she said to Annie,

"Now we have to think of how you are going to live."

"I'll manage somehow, dearie," Annie said in a tired voice.

"You have to manage only until I can send you some money from London," Petula said "and I promise you I shall not forget to do that. But first of all you have something left from what the Major gave you?"

"Something left?" Annie replied, "I should think I have, Miss Petula, I'm not throwin' good money away."

"Then keep it carefully and don't mention to my uncle that you have anything," Petula told her. "I am going to ask him to pay the bills we owe in the village before we leave and I think he can hardly refuse me."

"There be somethin' about him, smart though he appears, that makes me worry for you," Annie said slowly.

Petula thought that, if Annie knew the real truth, she would worry a great deal more, but, because she knew that there was nothing the old maid could do, she merely replied,

"Don't worry about me, Annie, I am worrying about you. I am going now to the farm."

"What for?"

"The rent is due at the end of March, as we all know, but Mr. Holbridge is always late, just as the others are. So I am going to collect it – myself."

"What you get from the tenants belongs to your uncle," Annie pointed out.

"Perhaps he will forget about it," Petula replied and hurried off to the farm.

When Sir Roderick returned an hour before dinnertime and swept through the front door, Petula knew that he had succeeded in what he had set out to do.

There was an expression of elation on his face and he put his arm round her shoulders and said,

"I have good news for you, my dear, very good news."

"You have sold The Manor and the estate?" Petula asked him in a small voice.

"I have sold it and sold it very well," he answered.

"Barrowick was dead keen, as you suspected, to become the Lord of the Manor. He had had to pay through the nose for the privilege, but he can well afford it."

"I am glad you are – pleased, Uncle Roderick."

"You can be pleased too," her uncle answered. "Now we can do things in style and that is the right word for it, Petula."

He looked at her in an appraising manner as he flung himself down onto a chair in the drawing room and smiled,

"I don't mind betting that, in a few weeks after you reach London, you will be the toast of St. James's."

Petula clasped her hands together.

"L-listen – Uncle Roderick, now you have the money you want, why not leave me a little – a very little of it and let me – stay here in Yorkshire. I shall be quite – happy with Annie in the cottage that Papa left her in his – Will."

"Left her a cottage?" Sir Roderick asked sharply. "You did not tell me that."

"I hardly realised it myself until I read Papa's Will. Shall I fetch it – for you?"

"Yes, let me have a look at it," her uncle urged at once.

Petula with her heart beating apprehensively fetched the Will from the library.

She put it into Sir Roderick's hands and he was silent while he read it.

"I see that it is only for her lifetime," he said at length, "and the same applies to the man, Adam. That will not alter the deal I have made with Barrowick."

"And what about my staying with Annie?"

"Can you be so childish and utterly insane as to wish to bury yourself here looking like you do?" her uncle asked. "My dear girl, I am going to put the world at your feet! The world of Bucks and Beaux, the world that centres around the Prince of Wales, who is the biggest Beau of them all. "

"I-I really don't want – that," Petula said and realised even as she spoke that her uncle was not listening to her.

"I promised to give you a halo of gold," he said with a grin on his lips, "and so that is just what you are going to have. Who is going to guess for one moment that it is Fairy gold, which cannot be touched by human hands?"

He laughed, but, as he did so, Petula shivered.

CHAPTER FOUR

"You were a great success last night, dear," the Honourable Mrs. Warren said to Petula in her gentle voice.

Petula smiled and was about to reply when her uncle demanded sharply,

"What did Lord Crowhurst say to you?"

"He paid me a lot of silly compliments," she answered him lightly.

Then, as she saw her uncle frown, she realised that she had said the wrong thing.

"Crowhurst is a very rich man," he retorted.

Petula wanted to add that he was also old, ugly and frightening.

But she had learnt by this time that it was a mistake to criticise and her uncle expected her to be amenable and submissive to everything he suggested.

She had in point of fact felt since she left Yorkshire as if she was being swept along by a typhoon, which left her breathless and at times unable to think clearly.

To begin with everything was new and bewildering and, although there was a great deal that was exciting, there were also a great many things that made her afraid and intimidated.

They had arrived in London and Sir Roderick had taken her to a small house in Islington that belonged, Petula found, to the Honourable Mrs. Warren.

Petula had learnt on her way down from the North that she was to be her chaperone. She was a sweet-faced woman nearing middle age and Petula had taken to her immediately.

"Mrs. Warren," her uncle explained, "belongs to one of the oldest families in England and her brother-in-law is Lord Warrancliff, a Gentleman-in-Waiting to the King."

It did not take Petula long to discover that Mrs. Warren was prepared to do anything her uncle asked because she was in love with him.

She also learned, though it took a little time to discover all the details, that Mrs. Warren's hope and prayer was one day to be married to Sir Roderick.

Unfortunately she had no money except what her husband had left her on his death.

This was enough to keep her in comparative comfort, but, if she married again, it would be taken from her and also the house she lived in.

As they neared London, Petula had asked her uncle,

"This lady who is to chaperone me – are you going to inform her that I am an heiress or will you tell her the – truth?"

"No one, and I mean no one, is to know anything except what I tell them about you," her uncle said positively.

He thought out more of the story and Petula soon learnt that she had only just come into so much wealth, which had been left to her by a relative on her mother's side who had made a great fortune in the West Indies.

"You don't have the handling of the capital," her uncle had said and she knew that he was inventing the story as he went along, "until you are twenty-five or you get married."

He said the last three words with an impressive note in his voice, which told Petula that this was the key to the whole masquerade.

"U-Uncle Roderick," she spoke to him in a worried voice, "what I do not – understand is, if I have such a large fortune, why should anyone rich wish to marry me? Surely it would be a poor man who would find me desirable?"

"You leave the poor men to me," her uncle said grimly. "I am very used to impecunious fortune-hunters. I can recognise them a mile off."

"But the rich men have their own money," Petula persisted.

Her uncle smiled cynically.

"No man is so rich that he does not wish for more and, what is even more important, he wants to be married for himself and not for what he possesses."

He smiled.

"It will be your job, Petula, to convince someone with money that it is of no consequence and that you love him as a man."

"But-but if I don't – love him?"

"Then you will pretend to," her uncle shouted at her. "You have to act out a part, Petula! Good God, every woman can act if she wants to."

He looked at her frightened eyes and added in a gentler tone,

"It will not be too difficult for you for, as your Guardian, I shall make it very hard for a man to be alone with you."

He let Petula absorb this statement before he added,

"Traditionally heiresses are kept strictly in golden cages and no one can open the door unless they can provide the key, which is a Wedding ring."

He laughed at his own fantasy and then went on.

"Leave everything to me, Petula. I realise that you are young and inexperienced, but that is at least ninety per cent of your charm. London men are satiated with sophisticated beauties who fall into their arms almost before they ask them to do so."

He looked her over in the calculating manner that she disliked before he said.

"You will be the unobtainable, or almost, and that will prove a real challenge."

Petula felt that she had no wish to be anything of the sort, but told herself that she was being extremely ungrateful especially as her uncle was so generous as regards clothes.

The day after they had arrived all the dressmakers came flooding in to the small house in Islington bringing with them sketches, patterns and even models of their gowns.

Everything they suggested was carefully scrutinised and appraised by Sir Roderick.

Petula's opinion was not asked and so she realised that he as well as Mrs. Warren were experts and the results of their choice were certainly inexpressibly lovely.

When they attended the first Reception that they had been invited to, Petula found that she was indeed the success that her uncle had envisaged.

How much was due to her appearance and how much to the stories that were already in circulation about her fortune was debatable.

The first thing Sir Roderick had done on arrival in London was to send a notice to *The Gazette* saying,

"*Sir Roderick Buckden, Baronet, has arrived in London from Yorkshire accompanied by his niece, Miss Petula Buckden, who is to make her curtsey at Buckingham Palace to Their Majesties. Sir Roderick Buckden has taken 47 Berkeley Square for the Season where he will entertain.*"

They had all moved to Berkeley Square from Mrs. Warren's small house in Islington as soon as Petula had collected enough new gowns to wear.

The house, she learnt, belonged in fact to one of Mrs. Warren's relations, who was ill in the country and was therefore prepared to rent it to Sir Roderick.

It was impressive, well-furnished and the right background, Petula knew, for an heiress.

Everything happened so quickly that it was only when she was all alone at night in the darkness of her room that she shivered and felt terrified of the future.

Sometimes she wanted to slip out of the house and find her way back to Annie and all that remained of the safety and security that she had once known and had relied on so much.

But she knew that the money she had left with her old Nanny would not last forever and that a rich husband would mean that she must support not only her uncle but also Annie and Adam.

Living so quietly in Yorkshire she had not realised that gentlemen could be so smart, so elegant and indeed so overwhelming.

Not in the way that the Major had been that was different, but in making her tongue-tied and stupid and wondering wildly how she could reply to the compliments they paid her.

'It is because I am so ignorant,' she decided.

At the same time the thought of having to marry any of the men whom she had met so far made her feel as if she was being dragged down into a quicksand from which there could be no escape.

One consolation was that Mrs. Warren was so kind and in her own way understanding.

"I know that this must seem a very strange life to you, dear," she said in her gentle way, "especially after your father was ill for so long and so you saw so few people while you were nursing him. But you will get used to it."

"I suppose so," Petula said, "but the men I sit next to at dinner talk about things I have never heard of and I cannot understand their jokes."

Privately Mrs. Warren thought that this was a good thing, but aloud she said,

"All you have to do is to look lovely and everyone is already acclaiming you as the most beautiful *debutante* of the whole Season."

"That is what Uncle Roderick – hoped I would – be."

"Your uncle is always right," Mrs. Warren said, "so just do as he says. He is so anxious for you to be a great success."

She wondered what Mrs. Warren would think if she knew what her uncle really desired. She felt ashamed that they must deceive this kind understanding woman as well as everyone else.

"What does it feel like to be a great heiress?" one of the gentlemen she had met last night had asked her.

"I still feel very much the same as I did before," Petula answered truthfully.

He laughed.

"You must not get your head turned by being in the position to buy anything that takes your fancy."

"I would hope not," Petula said.

"It is a very beautiful head whatever it does," he said, "but I am sure that you are tired of people telling you so."

"I only feel uncomfortable when I feel that they are being insincere," Petula retorted.

"Which I could never be," he answered gallantly.

He was about to say something else, then Sir Roderick joined them and in what seemed an obvious manner to Petula he drew her aside,

"That young man is of no use to you," he said, "so do not waste your time on him."

Petula felt it was horrible to think that she could only talk and be pleasant to someone if she was trying to get something out of them and in her case, a proposal of marriage.

Then she told herself that she was well aware, as her uncle was, that the money he had obtained from the sale of the house and the estate would not last for ever certainly not at the rate they were spending it, although it was only on what her uncle considered necessities.

"Will people think it strange, if I am so rich, that I do not give them expensive presents or subscribe generously to charities?" Petula had asked.

Her uncle laughed.

"The rich are usually very close-fisted," he replied, "they think it enough for you to be in their company without having to distribute largesse. Anyway a woman never has to put her hand into her pocket. Leave all that to me."

Petula thought that it was easy, considering she never had a penny of her own and even had to ask her uncle for money to place on the collection plate in Church on Sunday.

Again it was not the sort of Service she was used to, quiet and sincere, in the little grey stone Church in Buckden where she had been christened.

Everyone who was fashionable, she soon learnt, worshipped on Sunday morning at St. George's Church, Hanover Square in pews that were inscribed with their names and they paid a considerable rent for them.

It was really more of a fashion parade than a Church Service. The congregation greeted each other without lowering their voices.

The women inspected and criticised each other's gowns and Petula even heard several of the gentlemen exchanging racing tips.

It was hard to pray as she always had from the depths of her heart or talk to her mother, who she had always felt was especially near to her in Church.

When they walked down the aisle, she found herself sitting unaccountably beside Lord Crowhurst, who was asking when he could see her again.

As she might have easily expected, her uncle replied for her and she suddenly had the uncomfortable feeling that Lord Crowhurst was menacing her in a way that made her feel as if he was a dark cloud shutting out the sunshine.

"What are we doing today?" Mrs. Warren asked now as they sat in the morning room in the house in Berkeley Square.

It was a charming room overlooking a small paved garden at the back with a fountain playing in the spring sunshine.

"Crowhurst suggested that he would drive us down to Ranelagh," Sir Roderick replied.

Petula felt her heart drop.

"But I refused his offer," he went on. "Instead his Lordship is waiting impatiently to see Petula tonight when we go to the biggest ball we have been invited to so far."

"She must wear one of her prettiest gowns," Mrs. Warren exclaimed.

"Exactly," Sir Roderick agreed at once, "and, as I want both you ladies to look your best, I suggest you rest after I have taken you for a short drive in Hyde Park."

"That will be lovely!" Mrs. Warren exclaimed.

There was an expression in her eyes that told Petula how much she longed to be with her uncle.

"We are not tiring you too much, Elaine?" he asked her.

"No, of course not," she replied. "You know how exciting it is for me to go to all these parties, which I have refused ever since I was a widow because I had no escort."

Sir Roderick smiled at her and for a moment it seemed to Petula as if they had forgotten that she was in the room.

Then he rose to his feet and announced,

"Petula has undoubtedly made little ripples among the *Beau Monde*, but it is not enough. Tonight I intend her to meet Temple Coombe."

"The Earl?" Mrs. Warren questioned in a puzzled tone.

"The Earl indeed!" Sir Roderick repeated. "He has been a widower for five years and is desperate to have an heir."

"But he is far too old – " Mrs. Warren began.

They talked, Petula thought, as if she was not there and had no part in what was being planned for her. Because she felt that she could not bear it, she slipped away from the room and neither Sir Roderick nor Mrs. Warren seemed to be aware that she had left them.

As she walked up the finely carpeted staircase to her bedroom, she was thinking not of whom she would meet this evening but of the Major.

There had hardly been a moment since they had left Yorkshire that he had not been in her thoughts and she compared him to every man she met to their disadvantage.

She had thought that perhaps he would be in London and she would see him if only from a distance.

Then she told herself firmly that he had said they would never meet again and she must accept that and not fight against what was obviously his final decision.

And yet he had kissed her! Every night she fell asleep pretending that she was in his arms and his lips were on hers.

Sometimes she dreamed of him and awoke to feel that sensation of wonder and glory that he had evoked in her and which it was impossible for her to forget.

'How can I ever feel like that for anyone else?' she asked herself despairingly.

Then she told herself that she had to accept the fact that it had been a dream, a moment of enchantment that could never come to her again.

And yet inevitably as she dressed for the ball they were to attend, she wondered what the Major would say if he could see her in the exquisite gown that her uncle and Mrs. Warren had chosen for her to wear.

It was white, as was traditional for a young *debutante*, but with a difference in that it was trimmed with white camellias round the hem of the slim almost transparent skirt.

The new fashion, which had been introduced in Paris by the Empress Josephine and had only recently come to London, had both surprised and shocked Petula.

Never had she imagined in any way that a lady could reveal so much of her figure and yet be considered respectable.

Because she was slim and graceful, the high-waisted gowns that had something Grecian in their flowing lines made her look like a young Goddess.

When artificial camellias had been affixed to her hair, she might have posed for a statue of Aphrodite.

Mrs. Warren in a gown the colour of parma violets and wearing just a small tiara, looked very aristocratic. While Petula was bound to admit that her uncle in his evening clothes made most of his contemporaries look heavy and older in years than their age.

The expensive carriage that her uncle had hired for the Season was drawn by two well-bred horses and the coachman and footman in cockaded hats afforded them an air of distinct affluence.

'If people only knew the real truth,' Petula thought as she had thought a thousand times before.

Then she told herself that it was silly to keep worrying that they might be found out and exposed.

If they were, she was quite certain that her uncle would find a very plausible explanation as to why suddenly she had ceased to be an heiress.

She had learnt how cleverly he had spread the rumour of her wealth.

"When your uncle came into White's Club," one of his friends had said to her, "to throw himself down in a chair and say, 'I wager a monkey that not one of you will be able to guess what has happened to me,' we all laughed."

"One or two of us hazarded a suggestion," he went on.

He saw that Petula was listening to him and continued,

"Then your uncle exclaimed, 'you are all wrong! You see before you the Guardian, the protector and the administrator of the huge fortune of the most incredibly beautiful girl I have ever seen'."

"Of course we were curious," the storyteller continued, "And then he told us that he had brought you to London for the Season."

"Uncle Roderick has been very kind to me," Petula said feeling that some response was expected from her.

"There is no reason why he should not be," came the answer.

She knew from the dry note in the voice of her uncle's friend that he was thinking that Sir Roderick was enjoying living luxuriously as he had been unable to do in the past.

Now that she had been in London for over a week Petula could understand how the story her uncle had told in White's Club had spread swiftly round all the other Clubs and amongst the influential ladies who led Society.

As soon as they moved into Berkeley Square, invitations began to arrive.

Over some of them Mrs. Warren shook her head.

"They are not the sort of people who Petula should know," she would say gently.

Immediately Sir Roderick would tear up the invitation and throw it into the wastepaper basket.

"Should we not refuse formally?" Petula asked him.

"I will not even waste the writing paper on them," her uncle retorted.

Other of the invitations, however, made him smile with pleasure.

"I never thought that I would be invited to the Lennoxes," he said to Mrs. Warren. "It is amazing how the mere smell of money greases the wheels."

"You must not be so cynical," Mrs. Warren replied. "You know as well as I do that the Marquis has four unmarried sons and the eldest will inherit everything."

Sir Roderick had handed the invitation to Petula.

"Accept with pleasure," he ordered her.

When Mrs. Warren left the room, he added.

"You need not be in the least interested in the young men who the party is being given for. Concentrate on their friends."

His remark made Petula feel embarrassed and contributed to her shyness.

She was not aware that, because she looked so young, shy and innocent, men found her irresistible.

They gravitated towards her not just because they thought she was so rich, but because she seemed a little helpless and in need of protection.

"I may be a fool in many ways," she heard her uncle say once to Mrs. Warren, "but I am an infallible judge of horses and women. I knew the moment I first saw Petula that she was a winner and I am right."

"You are indeed," Mrs. Warren replied. "All those Dowagers tonight were saying how sweet and modest she is and not in the least uppish or pretentious because she has such a large fortune."

She smiled at Petula as she spoke and added,

"I would like to tell you, dearest child, what a pleasure it is to chaperone someone who is admired not only by the gentlemen but by the ladies as well."

Petula blushed and once again she had wondered what Mrs. Warren would think if she knew the truth and realised that she was helping a trickster to deceive those who were only being kind.

It certainly did not trouble her uncle, but it troubled her.

"Will the Prince of Wales be present tonight?" Mrs. Warren asked as the carriage drove from Berkeley Square down one of the streets that led towards Park Lane.

"Of course," Sir Roderick replied at once, "so do make yourself pleasant, Elaine, to Mrs. Fitzherbert. I know you do not really approve of her. At the same time she is a nice woman."

"There are a great many people who are shocked by her liaison with the Prince," Mrs. Warren pointed out in a rather prim voice.

"Well, I am not one of them and I don't wish you to be either," Sir Roderick replied.

Mrs. Warren did not answer.

Petula had learned that she could not have come to London at a better time to enjoy the entertainments and excess of the London Season.

After nine years of War the Amiens Treaty had brought a cessation of hostilities between France and England and not only Society but the people as a whole rejoiced at the return of peace and plenty.

Houses that had been shuttered and closed because the Master or the oldest son was with his Regiment were now open again.

The Prince of Wales at Carlton House set an obvious example of lavish entertaining and extravagance that was followed by all those who wished to be in the fashion.

Outside the huge mansion where they would be entertained tonight Petula saw the long stream of painted carriages drawn by horses with silver bridles and manned by servants in the most gorgeous gold-braided Livery.

There were linkmen with flaring torches and flunkeys in their powdered wigs outside the porticoed door and a red carpet spread up the steps and into a brilliantly lit hall.

Here waiting to proceed up the double staircase was a crowd of guests more splendidly dressed and sumptuously bejewelled than Petula had ever seen at any previous party.

Chandeliers glowing with a thousand candles heated the rooms and there was the heavy fragrance of flowers and the scent of exotic Parisian perfumes to make the air seem almost stifling.

The chatter of voices and the laughter of the ladies seemed to mingle with the glitter of the decorations and the sparkle of tiaras that were almost like crowns on every fashionably dressed head.

If to Petula it was a spectacle, to Sir Roderick it was a conclave of friends. He seemed to know everyone present and introduced Petula to so many people that she felt bewildered even before they had begun to climb the staircase.

There was no doubt that the surroundings were a perfect background for the guests.

There were pictures which she felt certain were priceless masterpieces and, when they reached the top of the staircase, there was furniture that she longed to examine as they moved on towards the open doors of what was obviously a huge salon.

And now she could hear the stentorian tones of the Master of Ceremonies announcing the guests.

"Viscount and Viscountess Loftus. His Excellency the Russian Ambassador and Princess de Lieven. The Earl and Countess of Berkeley."

Then their turn came.

"The Honourable Mrs. Warren, Miss Petula Buckden and Sir Roderick Buckden."

Mrs. Warren was busy shaking hands with a distinguished white-haired woman wearing a diamond tiara and a huge necklace of different stones.

"How lovely to see you again, dear Elaine. I am so delighted that you have brought Miss Buckden with you. I have heard so much about her."

She held out a gloved hand to Petula as she spoke who sank in a low curtsey.

"I do hope you will enjoy your first Season," her hostess said kindly. "You must meet my daughter, Emelye, who has just arrived in London."

Petula shook hands with a rather attractive girl, taller than she, who had a surprisingly hearty hand-grip and whose face was unmistakably sun-tanned.

"I hear you come from Yorkshire," she then said. "It is strange that we have never met, do you not think so, Adrian?"

She turned her head as she spoke to the man standing next to her in the receiving line and automatically Petula looked at him at the same time.

Suddenly she felt as if she had been turned to stone and it was impossible to breathe or move.

It was the Major who stood there, tall, overwhelming, seeming to dwarf everything and everyone by his mere presence.

Far away and so faintly that she could hardly hear what was being said, the girl who was called 'Emelye' was saying,

"Let me introduce you to my fiancé, the Duke of Donchester – Miss Petula Buckden."

Almost as if someone invisible forced her to bend her knees, Petula curtseyed and the man facing her bowed.

She could not put out her hand to touch his and she felt, as he did not move, that he too was finding it hard to breathe.

For a moment Petula met his eyes.

Then, as if it was all happening a very long way away, she realised that Mrs. Warren was waiting for her and so she moved on.

She could not see the crowded room or the people who packed it.

She felt as if everything was swimming in front of her eyes, covered by a mist so that it was impossible to distinguish anything or anyone.

"Are you all right?" Mrs. Warren asked her. "You look very pale."

"I-I think it is – the heat," Petula managed to reply.

Mrs. Warren led the way across the room to an open window.

"It is very stifling on the stairs," she said sympathetically, "but then you will be all right in a moment."

"Y-yes – yes of course," Petula murmured.

"Would you like your uncle to fetch you a glass of water?"

"No thank you, no I am – all right,"

As if to give her time to fight what must be a slight faintness, Mrs. Warren looked down into the garden below.

"How pretty it is with the fairy lights," she said. "One might almost be in the country."

Her words made Petula at once think of the wood where the Major had kissed her.

The sun had been percolating through the green leaves of the silver birch trees and it had been part of the glory and wonder of his kiss.

He had said that they would never meet again, but he was here, here in this room and he was engaged to the girl who had given her a hearty handshake, the girl with the suntanned face.

Her uncle joined them and there was a series of further introductions.

She did not hear their names, she did not know what they said to her or what she replied.

Later they moved from the Reception room down yet another staircase to the ballroom, a large room built but at the back of the house and opening onto the garden.

Petula danced, but all the time she was watching the door waiting to see one person and one person only.

Then and she was not certain how it had happened, she found herself in the garden with Lord Crowhurst.

"At last I have you to myself," he was saying in his thick voice.

"I-I think Uncle Roderick is looking for me," Petula countered automatically.

"Forget your uncle," Lord Crowhurst replied. "I want to talk to you without him always giving me the answers to my questions."

Petula realised that they were standing by the branches of a tree lit by hanging Chinese lanterns.

They were not far from the ballroom and there were couples either talking or walking all around them so that she was not afraid.

She only felt it was an unutterable bore to have to listen to this man when she wanted to think and she wanted to understand just why Major Adrian Chester was in reality the Duke of Donchester.

'No wonder he looked so aloof and disdainful when I first saw him in the garden,' she thought, 'but afterwards – '

She closed her eyes for a moment and heard Lord Crowhurst say with a note of concern in his voice,

"I did not mean to upset you and I only wanted you to know how much you mean to me already."

Petula put out her hand as if to find something to hold on to and he guided her to a seat directly beneath the tree.

"It is the heat," he said. "People always ask too many guests and then the whole thing is an intolerable crush as it is at Carlton House. I will fetch you a glass of champagne."

He moved away as he spoke and Petula closed her eyes, grateful he had gone because she wanted to think.

"Petula!"

There was no mistaking the voice that spoke to her and then her eyes opened to find him towering over her, his dark head silhouetted against a Chinese lantern.

Automatically she rose to her feet and felt him take her hand in his.

"I must speak to you."

She looked over her shoulder.

"Lord Crowhurst has – gone to fetch me some – champagne."

Without speaking to her the Duke drew her round the back of the tree and over the lawn towards some shrubs that were deep in shadow.

Only when they were out of range of the lanterns and there were only a few Fairy lights near them did he stop.

He had taken her hand, but now he released it and she raised her eyes to his face which she could see quite clearly by the light of the moon that was now climbing up the sky.

"Why are you here?" the Duke asked.

His voice sounded accusing and Petula answered quickly,

"Please – I beg of you – don't say that we have met or where you – found me. Uncle – Roderick will be very – angry if you do so."

"I understand now that your uncle is Sir Roderick Buckden," he said, "but I did not connect him with you when I came to The Manor. I don't know him well, but he is a member of my Club."

It was almost as if he was speaking to himself to clarify in his own mind what he knew and Petula murmured,

"You said we would – never m-meet again."

"But we have met, Petula, and I am trying to ascertain what has happened."

"You must not ask questions," she said quickly. "I did not – tell Uncle Roderick you had stayed at The Manor – therefore no one must ever – know about me please."

"But you will tell me."

She shook her head.

"Why not?" he asked.

Petula drew in a deep breath.

"Because the – man who came was a – Major who had been in the – Army."

"That was true enough," the Duke said, "I was indeed a Major in the Army and, when I am travelling, it is easier to do so incognito."

"It – must be, but – "

He saw in her eyes what she wanted to say and he asked almost abruptly,

"How could I know that the wheel of my phaeton would be damaged and I would meet you? I have tried to forget you, Petula, but it has been impossible."

She did not reply and after a moment he said in a different tone,

"Have you thought about me?"

As if he compelled her to answer, Petula replied in a voice he could hardly hear.

"Y-yes – "

"Often?"

"All – all the – time."

She saw a sudden light in his eyes.

"How then can you ask me to forget?"

"It was – a dream, as you said – and we had to somehow go back to – reality."

"But this is real and you are here."

"I know – but –"

"But! But! But!" he said. "I know what you are thinking, and I am thinking the same, but I could not help it, Petula. I lay awake for all that night wanting you so unbearably that all the willpower and self-control in the world could not prevent me from coming to find you."

He paused and looked down at her, at her eyes in the moonlight seeming to glow with a light that came from within and that made her radiate a strange enchantment, which swept what he was about to say from his lips.

"How could I have anticipated for one moment that this would happen to me?" he asked hoarsely.

"What do you – mean?"

"I mean that I fell in love. I fell in love with you and God knows, although I have tried, I cannot get you out of my mind or out of my heart."

He thought that it was impossible for any woman to look as beautiful as Petula when transformed by his words,

"Y-you – love me?"

She hardly breathed the words and yet he heard them.

"I love you," he replied, "I knew it before I kissed you, but, when I felt your lips meet mine, I knew that we belonged to each other. Yet there was nothing, believe me, Petula, there was nothing I could do about it."

"I – love you too," she whispered. "I was – afraid to admit it but, that is what I have been feeling – love. And it is – so entirely different from what I – expected."

"My precious! *My darling*!" he exclaimed. "Oh, God, how much I love you!"

He did not move, but she felt that he drew nearer to her and almost instinctively she put up her hands as if to ward him off.

"I will not touch you," he said, "though Heaven knows it is a hell not to do so, but I have to see you. Where are you? Where can we meet?"

"Uncle Roderick – " Petula began.

"I *have* to see you," the Duke interrupted. "I have to talk to you. There is so much to explain and yet I feel that you already understand."

He looked across the garden almost as if he felt that people were encroaching upon them.

"I must go back," he said, "and so must you, but tell me where we can meet at anytime, anywhere."

"I-I could slip out very early tomorrow morning, about five o'clock," Petula said, "but I don't know where – to suggest I should – go."

She spoke helplessly and the Duke moved a step forward as if he would take her in his arms to protect her.

Then he suggested,

"I will be waiting for you in a closed carriage at the corner of Curzon Street. Just walk around the corner of Berkeley Square and get into it."

His voice sharpened as he went on,

"If they discover that you have left the house, we will have to think up some explanation, but come to me, for God's sake, Petula! Come to me or I think I shall go mad!"

"I will – come," she promised.

Then it seemed as if he faded away into the shadows and left her so quickly that for a moment she thought that he was not real, but she had dreamed his presence beside her.

Then, as she moved back to the tree with the Chinese lanterns, she saw Lord Crowhurst with a glass in his hands looking for her.

CHAPTER FIVE

Soon after dawn Petula climbed out of bed and dressed.

She had not been able to sleep despite the fact that they had come home early.

Her uncle had been angry with her. Just as she joined Lord Crowhurst, he had come from the house with a black look on his face which told her that he was incensed.

"Where have you been, Petula?" he asked sharply. "There was someone I wished you to meet and I could not find you."

"It was so hot, Uncle Roderick," Petula began, only to be interrupted by Lord Crowhurst who said,

"I am afraid your niece felt faint, Buckden, and it is not surprising seeing that as usual there are far too many people crushed into far too small a space."

Her uncle did not answer, he merely took her by the arm and led her back towards the house.

As they neared the entrance, he said to her in a low voice,

"Surely you have enough sense to know that you should never go into the garden alone with a man?"

Petula did not reply.

It had been difficult enough ever since arriving at the ball and meeting the Duke to think about or concentrate on anything but him. Now she had talked to him it was doubly difficult.

Her uncle had introduced her to several people who were talking with Mrs. Warren and it was only later she realised that she had not heard their names nor could she even remember what they looked like,

She thought that she had talked to several other people, but she was not sure.

All she could think of was that the Duke loved her as she loved him.

'*He loves me,*' she whispered beneath her breath.

She felt herself thrill even though she recognised that he now belonged to the girl with the sun-tanned face.

At last after what seemed to be an interminable length of time she was back in her own bed and the room was in darkness.

Only then did she think that now she had found again the man who by his kisses had awoken such an ecstasy and glory within her, it would be even more agonising to lose him for the second time.

He loved her!

Over and over again she found herself remembering the deep note in his voice when he had said,

'*I fell in love with you and God knows, although I have tried, I cannot get you out of my mind and out of my heart.*'

'He loves me! Could anything, Petula asked herself, be more incredible, at the same time more utterly and – completely wonderful?'

She lay awake with her heart throbbing tumultuously in her breasts and she felt as if once again his lips were on hers in the quietness and beauty of the little wood when he had opened the Gates of Heaven to her.

As she dressed, she knew that nothing and nobody would stop her from going to him as he had asked her to do. Equally she was sure that she could leave the house unobserved.

In most London houses, especially those as grand as the one that her uncle had rented, there was always a footman and a nightwatchman on duty.

But then, as her uncle was economising in every possible way, that would not be noticed behind the grand façade he put on and the actual household consisted of few permanent staff.

When there was a dinner party, extra servants were hired for the occasion and so was the chef.

At other times there was just a plain cook who made no pretensions of doing anything elaborate, while an elderly man who had been trained as a butler and his wife kept the rooms comparatively clean.

None of them, Petula knew, would be about at this hour of the morning, although Annie had told her that in smart houses the under-housemaids and the kitchen staff were always up by five o'clock.

Wearing one of the plainest gowns she possessed, but which was still to her both lovely and elaborate, and a straw bonnet trimmed simply with blue ribbons, she slipped noiselessly down the staircase.

It was not difficult to slide back the bolts on the front door and she thought that, if Bruton, the butler, found them undone, he would suppose that he had been absent-minded the night before.

Berkeley Square was deserted.

Later it would be filled up with lavender-sellers, organ-grinders and crossing-sweepers besides, like every other street in London, a large number of beggars.

Many of them were maimed and crippled men who had been discharged from the Army and the Navy without being recompensed by the country they had fought so valiantly for.

It was a very short distance to Curzon Street and Petula hurried along, thinking it most unlikely that anyone would see her, but knowing that, if one of the neighbours did so, they would think it extraordinary that she was unchaperoned.

Then, as she rounded the corner, she saw a carriage waiting.

It was a small unostentatious brougham without painted panels or even identifiable by a Crest.

There were two men on the box and one of them jumped down as soon as she appeared.

As he opened the door of the carriage, she saw that it was Jason and he touched his hat as Petula, too shy to acknowledge him, stepped into the carriage.

A hand came out to assist her, the door closed behind her and almost immediately the horses moved off.

She half-turned to raise her eyes to the man beside her and realised that he was looking at her in the same searching manner.

"You came!" he almost shouted. "I was so afraid that something might stop you."

"I – wanted to see you."

She thought that her voice sounded strangely unlike her own, but then her whole body was pulsatingly aware of the Duke, of his closeness to her and that they were alone.

Because she was shy of her own emotions, she said in an effort to appear natural,

"You are – still in evening – dress."

He smiled.

"I had no time to change. My last guest only left about half-an-hour ago."

He saw the question in her eyes and added,

"Did you not know that it was my house you came to?"

"N-no – I did not know – I did not even know who had – invited us," Petula replied.

"You have to explain and you have to tell me what has happened," the Duke insisted.

As she did not answer, he went on,

"When I saw you tonight, I thought I must be dreaming, in fact I have dreamt of you so often that I find your face everywhere I look."

Petula quivered and he took her right hand in both of his and held it closely to his chest.

"You are more beautiful than I remember," he said, "and yet it would be impossible for anyone to be lovelier than you were when I kissed you in the wood."

She felt her fingers tremble in his.

"Petula, what has happened to us?" he asked. "And what are we to do about it?"

"What – can we do?"

She found it hard to breathe the words.

"Do you suppose I have not been thinking of every possibility since I left you standing on the steps looking so forlorn and lost? And at the same time so incredibly heartbreakingly beautiful."

Petula drew in her breath and then she said hesitatingly,

"Y-you are – to be – married!"

"I was on my way to Kirkby Castle," he replied, "for my engagement to be announced first to the Earl's relatives. Then we were all to return to London for the ball you attended last night."

He paused and she heard the pain sharp as a knife in his voice as he said,

"The announcement appears in *The Court Circular* this morning."

The pressure of his fingers on hers hurt as he went on,

"It is something that has been planned for years. In fact ever since I was twenty-one or perhaps before that. My father and the Earl were close friends."

"Do you – love her?"

The Duke knew that it was the one question Petula needed to ask.

"I am fond of Emelye," he answered, "and I have known her since I was a child. We have many tastes in common. She loves horses and so do I and she is a magnificent rider."

He saw the expression in Petula's eyes and added,

"But I have never been in love, my darling, and this is the truth, until I met you."

"Just how can we – love each – other?" Petula then asked him.

"Your question should be how can we help it?" he replied. "It happened so swiftly that I thought I must be imagining the whole thing."

He gave a deep sigh.

"Then, when I touched you and when I kissed you, I knew that all the stories about love at first sight, of being overwhelmed, bewitched and infatuated to the point of madness were all true."

"I-I felt exactly the same," Petula whispered, "but it is wrong because you – belong to – someone else."

"It is not wrong, my precious," the Duke said. "It is just that there seems to be nothing honourable I can do about it."

Petula turned her face to look directly at him and he asserted with a sudden violence,

"God Almighty, what am I to do? Give me the answer."

Because he frightened her a little, she would have taken her hand away from his, but he held onto it tightly.

"I am sorry. Forgive me," he asked her. "I cannot think of you and remain sane."

He raised her hand as he spoke in both of his and kissed it and she felt that indescribable sensation that he had aroused in her before rise in her breasts and into her throat.

"I love you!" he said, "and I do know when I look into your eyes, as I knew before I left your house, that you love me a little."

. "Yes – I love – you!" Petula murmured, "but you are – betrothed."

She felt as she spoke as if she had struck at him, but he kissed the back of her hand once again before still holding it in both of his.

"Now tell me about yourself," he said. "Last night when you were dancing Emelye said to me, 'that is the Yorkshire heiress who everyone is talking about. I cannot think why I have not met her. I thought, as Papa is Lord Lieutenant, I knew everyone I should in Yorkshire'."

Petula did not answer and the Duke carried on,

"Where did all this money come from? How could it have happened so quickly?"

"I-I cannot – tell you."

"Why not?"

"Because it is not only – my secret."

"Why should there be a secret?" the Duke asked. "When I saw your house, I realised that you were very poor, at least I thought so."

Petula was silent and after a moment he said,

"There cannot be any mysteries or secrets between us. Tell me, Petula, what happened."

"It is – better for you not to – know," she answered, "and, as you are well aware – we must not – see each other again."

"How can I bear it? How can I live knowing that you are in London and looking for you at every party I attend and at every place I go?"

"Then – perhaps I should go – away."

Even as she spoke she wondered wildly how she could achieve it. What would her uncle say after he had spent so much money on her clothes, the house and the whole masquerade?

"As I told you last night, I have met your uncle," the Duke said. "I know he is a gambler, who has not appeared to have much money until now. Where has it come from? And why are you spoken of as an heiress?"

"Please," Petula pleaded, "please – do not probe and ask questions. I don't want to tell you – why I am here, I do not – want you to know."

"What has happened to The Manor?" the Duke wanted to know.

Because the question took her by surprise, Petula told him the truth,

"Uncle Roderick – sold it."

She saw a speculative look come into the Duke's eyes and added quickly.

"Perhaps I should – not have said that. Please forget – it."

"I think I am beginning to understand," he said slowly. "Your uncle sold the house and the estate, then seeing how beautiful you are, he brought you to London."

His hands tightened on hers until she gave a little cry.

"What for?" he asked. "Tell me what for?"

The colour rose in Petula's cheeks, but she could not speak.

"I know the answer," he said bitterly, "for a rich husband! It is obvious, is it not?"

Once again his voice was violent.

"How could you do such a thing? How could you lower yourself to seek for a husband by such means?"

"I-I could not help it," Petula answered. "If I had not – done as Uncle Roderick said, he would have – left me to – starve."

The tears started to gather in her eyes and the Duke put his arm around her and pulled her against him.

"My sweet! My darling! I have made you cry. How can I be such a brute? I understand, of course, I understand, but how can I ever see you married to someone else?"

His arm holding her close against him gave her an inexpressible feeling of security and, without really meaning to do so, she put her head against his shoulder.

With his free hand he undid the ribbons of her bonnet and, pulling it from off her head, threw it onto the floor of the carriage.

Then he said, his voice low and tender.

"Let me look at you. I shall never forgive myself for having made you cry."

He wiped away the tears that had fallen onto her cheeks and then he said,

"Tell me everything for I have to know."

Hesitantly, at the same time feeling it was impossible to do anything but what he wished, Petula told him how her uncle had arrived at Buckden.

She related how he had sold the estate and, although she had suggested staying there with Annie, he had insisted that she should come to London so that he could find her a rich husband.

She knew by the way the Duke's arm tightened about her and the expression on his face as he listened that he was shocked and even appalled at her uncle's plan.

Equally there was a relief in knowing that at any rate she need not pretend to him.

When she finished speaking, he was silent and after a moment she said pathetically,

"Because of what I have – told you – you will not stop – loving me?"

"Do you really think that would be possible?" he asked. "If you committed murder, if you were accused of every crime in the calendar, I should still love you because I cannot help myself."

He looked into her eyes and sighed,

"When I drove away telling myself I must forget you, I left my heart behind."

"And you took – mine with – you," Petula whispered.

Slowly, as if it was inevitable, the Duke's lips found hers.

For a moment he was very gentle.

Then, as he had done before in the garden, he pulled her closer still and his kiss became demanding, insistent and utterly and completely possessive.

She knew that he held her captive. She was his and, where their feelings were concerned, there was no escape for either of them.

They belonged to each other and they were one person.

When the Duke raised his head, he thought that while Petula had been lovely before, at this moment she seemed to shine with an inner radiance that had something celestial about it.

"I love you!" he said hoarsely. "There are no other words to express what I feel."

"And I – love – you!" Petula answered and hid her face against his shoulder.

She felt him touch her hair gently and realised that the carriage had come to a standstill.

She turned her head and saw through the window that they had stopped by some trees at the side of the Serpentine.

There was no one about and it was very quiet.

The light of the early sun was percolating through the branches and shining on the silver water and made her think of the wood at Buckden and how it was there that she had first been aware of her love.

As if the Duke followed her thoughts, he said,

"I have thought about you every day and every night and, while I kept telling myself it was wrong to do so, I just knew that eventually it would be impossible for me not to return to you."

"It would be wrong – you are to be – married," Petula pointed out again.

"I know," the Duke replied, "but what can I do? My darling, my dream come true, tell me what can I do?"

"There is – nothing," Petula answered. "As you said yourself – nothing honourable."

"I torture myself that, if I had been brave enough to take you away with me, it might have been possible," the Duke said.

"They were waiting for you at Kirkby Castle?"

"Yes, and the Earl's relatives, of course, had already been told of the engagement before my arrival."

"Then there is nothing – you could have done."

"How could I have been such a fool?" he asked, "as to agree to a marriage without love? My only excuse is that I did not know that love such as I have for you existed except in the imagination of some poet."

He put his hand under Petula's chin and turned her face up to his.

"How can you be so absurdly lovely?" he said. "How can everything you say and do tug at the heart I did not know I possessed? How can your lips give me an awareness of the Heaven that I had ceased to believe in?"

"That is – what I feel about you," Petula said, "but I never – never dreamt that you would – feel the same."

"And now that you know I do?"

"I am proud – so very proud that you should – love me."

"But how can we exist without each other?"

He stared at the still water shining in the early sun as if he thought that it would give him a solution. Then, because she knew how desperate he felt, Petula said quietly,

"You must do what is – right. After all you are very important and I am – a nobody. It would damage your – reputation if we were talked – about."

"If we could be talked about, it would make me the happiest man in the world," the Duke insisted.

He gave another deep sigh and then he added,

"If you were really nobody, then it might be easier, but I knew at Buckden that the only position I could offer you in my life would be that of my wife."

Petula was silent for a moment and then she murmured,

"I-I think I understand. You mean – if I had really been a nobody you might have asked me to be your – mistress."

The Duke pulled her roughly against him.

"I would not spoil anything quite so perfect by such a suggestion. As I have already said, Petula, if it had been possible, I would have come back and asked if you would honour me by being my wife."

As he spoke, his lips found hers again and he kissed her until the world seemed to swing round her and she was unconscious of everything except for him and the wonder he evoked in her.

Finally, as he then released her, she could only look up at him with her breath coming brokenly through her parted lips and her eyes seeming to hold all the sunshine in their depths.

"I love – you! Oh, *I – love you*!" she cried and the Duke threatened,

"If you look at me like that, I shall carry you away with me here and now and damn the consequences!"

There was a growing passion in his words that did not make Petula afraid, but feel as if she vibrated to music.

Then she said,

"If you will not think of – yourself, I must think for – you. We must – say 'goodbye' – and we must try – to forget."

"That is impossible," the Duke asserted sharply. "Do you think I can forget that you are looking for a husband, that some other man will touch you, kiss you and make you his?"

He felt the quiver of revulsion that ran through Petula's whole body and countered,

"If it kills me to think of it, what will it do to you, my darling? For I know you love me and I know you belong to me spiritually."

"Perhaps I could – run away and hide – somewhere," Petula suggested.

"For the rest of your life?" he asked. "My precious, it would be impossible wherever you hid for some man not to see you. Even if he arrived unexpectedly after an accident to his phaeton!"

He had tried to smile, but instead there was an agony in his eyes that made Petula press herself a little closer to him as she said,

"We must not – regret. At least we have – known how wonderful – love can be. No one can take that – away from us."

"It may seem of some consolation to you," the Duke replied. "But I think that love has inflicted on me a torture more intense and crueller than I could ever express in words."

"No – please – " Petula protested at once, "you must not – think like that. If I had never – met you, if you had never – kissed me, I should not have – known that love is the most – perfect, the most – beautiful thing in the world and part – of God Himself."

The Duke made a little sound that was almost like a broken cry.

Then he held her close against him, his lips on her hair, his eyes looking unseeingly at the shining water of the Serpentine.

For a moment Petula pretended that they were together and that no one could separate them.

Then she forced herself to say in a voice hardly above a whisper,

"I think – I must go – back."

"I would not get you into trouble," the Duke said, "but, darling, I must see you again very soon."

Petula shook her head.

"I may – harm you."

"You are thinking of me!" he said. "My precious, was there ever anyone like you?"

"I love you so!" Petula replied. "But, because you are a Duke, because you are of such importance, you must not do anything which would shock people or make them sneer at you. I could not – bear it. I could not bear to be a – part of that."

"If you are thinking of me, then I am thinking of you," he said, "and, my darling, of the sort of husband your uncle will choose for you."

Petula thought of Lord Crowhurst and turned her face so that the Duke could not see the expression in her eyes.

"I have no right to ask questions," he said, "except that you have given me the right because you love me."

He paused before asking,

"Is there nothing I can do? Suppose I gave you some money? Would that make things any better?"

Petula shook her head.

"How could I explain where the money has come from? And we must not, as you know, be – involved with – each other."

"But we *are* involved!" the Duke emphasised fiercely.

"Only in our hearts," Petula answered quietly. "Our minds know that you already belong to – someone else. Papa always said that once a man gave his word as a gentleman it was impossible for him to break it."

"Your father was right," the Duke agreed. "But at the same time this is different."

He smiled cynically as he went on,

"What man does not say that when he is in love? But this is different! It is different, my precious darling, because we were made for each other and because already you belong to me and I to you."

Petula did not answer him and, as if he knew that it was all hopeless, the Duke offered,

"I will take you back."

He tapped on the front of the carriage and immediately the horses began to move.

Petula looked for a moment at the trees and the water of the Serpentine and thought that this was another enchanted place she would always remember because the Duke had kissed her there.

Then the horses were carrying them back through Hyde Park, across Park Lane and into Curzon Street.

They sat in silence, the Duke holding her closely against his chest. And she knew that his chin was squared and his lips set in a tight line as they had been when he had driven away from The Manor and left her behind.

Only as the carriage came to a standstill in Curzon Street did he say,

"And I shall be thinking, thinking of some way out of this muddle, but God alone knows what it will be."

"1 shall be – thinking of – *you*," Petula said softly.

"You will take good care of yourself?" he asked anxiously.

She found it impossible to speak because tears were misting her eyes.

She picked up her bonnet and put it on her head, then the Duke tied the ribbons under her chin.

His eyes looked at her hungrily and she thought the lines on his face were sharply drawn.

Then he raised her hand and laid it against his cheek, not kissing it, only holding it there.

Jason opened the door and without speaking, without even looking back, Petula stepped out.

She had already planned not to enter the house by the front door but from the Mews.

She realised that the coachman her uncle had hired would not be particularly interested in anything she did.

As she walked over the cobblestones with the stables on either side of her, she could hear the horses moving in their stalls and the grooms whistling as they rubbed them down.

She found the door that led into the Mews of No. 47.

There was a passage running alongside the stalls and a door opened into another passage, which led directly to the kitchen quarters of the house.

As she had already anticipated, there was no one about and she slipped up the back stairs and found her way to her bedroom.

There she undressed and climbed back into bed.

Only when she could hide her face in the pillows did she begin to cry helpless, agonising tears that seemed to come from her very soul.

*

"Sir Roderick would like to see you, miss, as soon as you are dressed," Tomkins, who was Petula's lady's maid, told her as she took away her breakfast tray.

She was experienced and therefore more expensive than any of the other servants in the household. But she was, Petula had found, a genius at arranging her hair and looking after her gowns.

"I had better get up," Petula said quickly.

"There are no engagements until after luncheon, miss," Tomkins related, "so one of your simpler gowns will do."

Petula was not listening, but she was merely wondering why her uncle should wish to see her. Perhaps it concerned her behaviour of the night before.

It was always difficult for him to talk to her in front of Mrs. Warren just in case he said something that would reveal the part that they were both playing.

Usually he drew her aside with the pretence that he had some papers for her to sign, but it was unusual for him to send messages so early in the morning.

'Perhaps he is really – angry with me,' Petula told herself and felt her heart sink.

She felt weak with the emotions she had experienced and then the violence of her tears.

She washed her face very carefully, first in warm water, then in cold and hoped that her uncle would not realise that she had been crying.

Tomkins arranged her hair and she went downstairs to find Sir Roderick as she expected in the library.

He was looking very smart, for he too had bought some new clothes, but one glance at his expression told Petula that he was not angry as she had feared but in a good humour.

"Good morning, Petula," he began. "I hope you enjoyed yourself last night?"

"Yes, indeed, Uncle Roderick. It was a very magnificent party."

"So I suppose it was sheer ignorance that made you go into the garden alone with Lord Crowhurst. You knew as well as I do that you are not supposed to be alone with a man."

"I am very sorry – Uncle Roderick – it was so hot – and I felt a little faint."

"I understand," Sir Roderick said, "but don't let it happen again."

"No, Uncle Roderick."

"What I want to tell you is that, whilst you should keep Crowhurst on a string, so to speak, we have a better fish to fry."

Sir Roderick laughed.

"It sounds rather vulgar, but it expresses quite eloquently what I am trying to say."

"I don't – understand."

"Well, Temple Coombe, as I anticipated, is extremely interested in you."

Petula looked at him blankly.

After all the people she had met last night, she was trying to recall which was the Earl of Temple Coombe.

Because she had been thinking only of the Duke, every face was just a blur and it was impossible even to remember anything that anyone had said to her.

"Come along, Petula, don't be so stupid," Sir Roderick admonished her. "The Earl of Temple Coombe may be slightly old, I am not denying that, but he is an extremely important man in a number of ways and, if you could bring him up to scratch, which I believe you will, then we are home and dry!"

"I am – afraid I don't remember the – gentleman."

Sir Roderick made a sound of exasperation.

"I introduced him to you after you came back from the garden. He was standing with a number of other people including Mrs. Warren. If you had been attending, which you should have been, you would have felt me press your arm. Really, Petula, at times I do think you are half-witted!"

"I am sorry – Uncle Roderick."

"I suppose I must excuse you as you were not feeling well, but frankly, this is no time for illness."

"No, no – I am very – sorry."

"I will forgive you because we are dining with the Earl tonight."

Sir Roderick was obviously elated.

"His servant brought the invitation early this morning, which shows that he is keen."

"I am glad you are pleased, Uncle Roderick."

"Pleased? *I am elated*! This is exactly what I had planned. Everything is going perfectly. As I have said before, I sensed what I must do where you were concerned. And I was right yes, by God, I was right!"

Sir Roderick walked over to a desk and, opening one of the drawers, took out a small notebook.

"You will see how carefully I have planned a campaign like this, Petula," he said. "I put down in this little book the names of half-a-dozen men whom I intended you should meet in London."

He looked at the book with a smile on his lips as he went on,

"Only one of them has proved to be a non-starter. There is Crowhurst already at your feet, Temple Coombe, who you will see tonight, and that leaves three others, all members of White's, who have already said that they would like to have the opportunity of meeting you."

He threw the book down on the desk and added smugly,

"You are lucky to have a very clever uncle."

"Yes – of course – Uncle Roderick," Petula agreed, "and I am indeed very – grateful."

She tried to enthuse the proper responsive note into her voice, but it was hard.

"You are looking tired," Sir Roderick commented sharply. "There are lines under your eyes that I have not noticed before. You had better rest this afternoon."

"Have you forgotten, Uncle Roderick, that Mrs. Warren is taking me to the – Drawing Room at St James's Palace?"

"Good Heavens so I had," Sir Roderick exclaimed. "Well, you certainly cannot miss it, and that reminds me, I am due at a Levée tomorrow morning. They say the King has actually recovered enough to take them himself."

He walked back to stand in front of the mantelpiece as he went on,

"Remember that St James's is exceedingly formal. The King and Queen may live quietly at Windsor, but everything is very much *de rigueur* in London."

He paused for a moment and then remarked,

"Court dress is compulsory and both the King and the Queen are stuffily Royal on such occasions. Needless to say the whole performance is excessively boring."

"I am sure I shall find it interesting, Uncle Roderick."

"Doubtless you will," Sir Roderick agreed, "but, as far as I am concerned, I enjoy myself a great deal more with the Prince of Wales, however much His Majesty condemns his son's behaviour."

Petula was next wondering in which camp the Duke found himself.

She had learnt as soon as she had come to London that, while everything social which was amusing and entertaining centred around the Prince of Wales at Carlton House, the more important aristocrats allied themselves with the King and Queen.

Even so they all admitted, as her uncle did, that the parties at Buckingham Palace, like those at St James's Palace, were extremely dull.

'Perhaps the Duke manages not to ally himself with either group,' Petula thought.

She felt herself aching at the thought of how important he was and how hopeless it was to love someone so unfortunately above her in every way.

Only when she escaped from her uncle and was alone could she forget everything but the fact that the Duke loved her as she loved him.

It was a joy and an agony in one.

It was a rapture, at the same time a deep dark despondency, to know that she could never be a part of his life or he of hers.

Perhaps, she now thought, they would both be happier if she disappeared from the Social scene and became his mistress.

Then she realised that such a thought was wicked and would have horrified her mother. Yet, as the Duke had said, could such a love as they had for each other ever be wrong?

Love, real love, came, Petula was sure, from God and it was God, not chance, who had brought them together.

It was God who had made what they both felt for each other so perfect and so Divine that she knew that it was part of everything she had ever believed was sacred.

'I love him!' she told herself. 'And my love is great enough to want his happiness and to know that I must not harm him in any way. Even if it means that I must never see him again.'

The pain of such a thought was almost intolerable and yet she knew she must be strong enough for both of them.

Strong enough to know that they had said 'goodbye' and there was nothing more that they could say to each other.

In the afternoon, with powdered hair and wearing Court dresses with hoops, panels and draperies that were so very different from the slim gauzes and muslins that were the fashion, Mrs. Warren and Petula drove towards St James's Palace.

It had seemed to Petula a terrible waste of money that they should have to spend so much on gowns that they would never wear again after this one occasion when she was to make her curtsey to the Queen.

But then it was all part of Sir Roderick's plan that she should be formally accepted as a *debutante*.

Petula learnt that a large number of the invitations she had received were due to the fact that after today she would be accepted in Court circles.

"It is quite some years now since I have been to St. James's Palace," Mrs. Warren related reminiscently.

"What was the last occasion?" Petula asked her.

"I was presented on my marriage."

"Were you very happy with your husband?"

Mrs. Warren hesitated for a moment before she responded,

"My marriage was arranged by my father and my husband was much older than I was."

There was a note in her voice that told Petula now why she had protested yesterday when Sir Roderick had been talking about her meeting Lord Temple Coombe.

"So was it much more – difficult to be married to an – older man than to a younger one," Petula asked.

Again Mrs. Warren paused before she replied,

"Older men, especially if they have never been married before, are very set in their ways. At the same time I expect you know the ancient adage that '*it is better to be an old man's darling than a young man's slave*'."

Petula wanted to say that she really longed to be a slave to the man she loved, but she said nothing and after a moment Mrs. Warren went on,

"I know, dearest child, that your uncle is very anxious for you to marry and settle down. I have tried to persuade him that there is no need to hurry, but you know how impetuous he is."

"Yes – indeed," Petula answered.

"As you are so well endowed, you should be able to take your time and find someone you love."

Petula did not speak and after a moment Mrs. Warren continued,

"If there is anyone that you love, even if he does not meet with your uncle's approval, I will try to help you for I wish you to be happy."

Petula felt that instinctively, because she was a woman, Mrs. Warren sensed that she was in love.

She had a sudden impulse to tell her the truth and beg for her help.

Then she knew that it would do her no good and would only infuriate her uncle and his plans.

Mrs. Warren was almost as poor as they were and was therefore not in a position to help. Besides how could anyone alter the impossible situation where she loved a man who was to be married to someone else?

'It is hopeless – *hopeless*!' Petula told herself.

She realised that, if she could not marry the Duke, then it did not really matter who she married for any other man would seem intolerable to her in the circumstances.

They arrived at St James's Palace and were led by a resplendent official up the wide oak staircase to the Reception rooms.

Here in similar fashion to themselves with panniers and heavy trains hanging from their shoulders, were the other ladies waiting either to be presented or to present their daughters.

The majority of them seemed to know Mrs. Warren and Petula found herself curtseying and repeating over and over again how much she was enjoying her first Season in London.

Then, as Mrs. Warren moved away from one old acquaintance to another, a voice said,

"I rather expected to find you here, Elaine. I do hope that you are not too tired after last night."

It was the Countess of Kirkby who was speaking and beside her Petula saw her daughter, Lady Emelye Kirk.

Then, as the two older women talked together, Lady Emelye said,

"Did you enjoy my party last night? Personally I thought it was all a terrible crush and would much rather have been in Yorkshire."

"I have not been to many balls," Petula replied shyly, "but everyone said it was the most fashionable and by far the best that has been given so far."

"I prefer riding to dancing," Lady Emelye admitted. "Do you ride?"

"Yes, when I am in the country. I have not yet ridden in London."

"I should not bother," Lady Emelye said scathingly, "it is very tame, trit-trotting in the Park. Papa has a miniature Racecourse at Kirkby and I train my horses over the jumps."

"That must be very exciting," Petula tried to enthuse.

"If you should want to buy some really decent hunters you had better come and see what we can show you. We have been breeding for some years and have produced some very fine horseflesh."

She did not seem to realise that Petula had found little to say and after a moment went on,

"Well, thank goodness I can go back to Yorkshire the day after tomorrow. I find all this sort of thing a terrible bore as I expect you do."

Petula was saved from answering because at that moment two Officers of State in Court uniform holding their staves of Office walked into the room backwards.

The Queen was arriving!

There was a hush that was almost one of awe, but Petula could only think that, if Lady Emelye was leaving London, then doubtless the Duke would go with her.

All her previous resolutions were cast away and she knew that somehow by some means she must see him alone just once more.

CHAPTER SIX

"I have not had a chance to talk to you until now," Sir Roderick said. "While Crowhurst has intimated clearly that he desires to marry you, Temple Coombe is still hanging fire."

He had called Petula into the library after she and Mrs. Warren had returned to the house from shopping.

Petula stood just inside the door looking, although she was unconscious of it, extremely lovely in a new gown of pale green which made her look like spring itself.

She did not speak and after a moment Sir Roderick suggested reflectively,

"Perhaps you should give him a little more encouragement, although your recent quiet, rather detached attitude has been, I admit, extremely effective."

He walked across the room while speaking as if it encouraged him to think and he went on,

"So many people have congratulated me on your modest demeanour and, though at first I thought it a mistake for you to seem so distrait, it has, I must confess, been very successful."

Petula knew that he was referring to the fact that she had hardly seemed aware of what was happening around her.

He was, of course, unaware that she could think only of one person and that was the Duke, who was to marry Lady Emelye Kirk.

It seemed as if no one could talk about anything else. Even Mrs. Warren discussed the engagement incessantly and then Petula found it hard to behave as if she was not personally interested.

"The Countess has always been a friend of mine," she told Petula, "and I am so delighted that their only child should make such an advantageous match."

"I hear that she has known the Duke for a long time," Petula said since Mrs. Warren was obviously expected her to say something.

"Yes, indeed, ever since they were children. But I think my friend was slightly afraid that he might cry off. There have been, as you might imagine, a great many women in love with him."

Mrs. Warren laughed.

"But, as they were usually sophisticated Society beauties who already had husbands, the Duke has been preserved for Emelye."

"She – is very – lucky," Petula said and hoped that her voice did not sound envious.

"She is indeed. The Duke of Donchester is not only extremely wealthy and he owns the most magnificent houses, like the one you saw the other evening, but he is also a very brave man."

"Brave?" Petula questioned.

"Yes, certainly," Mrs. Warren replied to her. "The Colonel of his Regiment was saying the other night what an excellent Officer he was and besides that the Duke is a

Corinthian and his success on the turf appeals to Emelye who is an outstanding rider."

Mrs. Warren's voice was full of admiration as she finished,

"Her mother has told me that in Yorkshire she is acclaimed as the best woman equestrian anyone has ever seen."

Petula knew that Mrs. Warren enjoyed praising the daughter of her friend.

But to her every word was like a dagger striking at her heart.

How could she compete, she asked herself, with somebody who fitted so admirably into the Duke's life?

Then she told herself severely that there was no question of a competition.

To her he was a real magical enchantment which had transformed them for one ecstatic moment, but which could never be anything in their lives but a dream.

Immersed in her own unhappiness she really paid no attention to the machinations of her uncle and all his plots and plans to marry her to the Earl of Temple Coombe.

The dinner party he had invited them to had not been the intimate affair that Sir Roderick was expecting.

Instead thirty people had sat down to a very long and tedious banquet and they had been joined afterwards by a number of other guests who gambled for high stakes at the tables that were arranged in one of the salons.

The majority of the gentlemen had been the same age of their host, which Petula found with something approaching horror was to her very old indeed.

She had thought Lord Crowhurst an elderly man, but the Earl was older still.

He had been distinguished-looking, if not handsome, in his youth, but now his face was lined, his hair grey and, although he held himself erect, she felt that it was with somewhat of an effort.

Nevertheless he was certainly not past the age of enjoying female company.

He flirted assiduously, Petula noticed, with the two beautiful women bedecked in jewels who sat on either side of him at dinner and there was a look in his eye when he talked to her which made her feel embarrassed.

Just as her uncle had done, she thought he appraised her as if she was a horse, but it was different in that she knew he was considering her in a very different capacity and her whole being shrank from the idea of him even touching her.

To her delight, however, she learnt that the Earl was leaving London the following day for Windsor Castle where he was to stay for the Ascot Races and she was therefore reprieved from coming into contact with him again until his return.

There was no doubt that her uncle, like a busy spider, was spinning his web and she felt as if she was a helpless little fly who had no chance of escaping from the silken threads by which he was holding her captive.

Now Sir Roderick said almost harshly,

"So if we cannot get Temple Coombe to say something definite by the end of next week, you will have to accept Crowhurst."

"Oh, no! Please – not, Uncle Roderick. Surely there could be – someone else – nicer than either of them?"

"Nicer?" her uncle queried at once. "They are both extremely wealthy."

"But-but they are – old and I cannot bear to be – near either of them."

It was the first time that Petula had spoken in such a positive way and her uncle looked at her in surprise.

"So you have some feelings after all?" he remarked.

"Of course I have feelings," Petula retorted, "but I am trying to behave as you wished me to do. Please – please do *not* make me marry either – Lord Crowhurst or the – Earl of Temple Coombe."

"And who are you hoping might take their place?" her uncle asked sarcastically. "The Prince of Wales? Or perhaps some Angel Gabriel we have not yet met. My dear Petula, let me make it clear once and for all that you cannot afford to be fastidious."

There was something in the way he spoke that made Petula look at him quickly.

"Have we spent – all the money you – obtained by selling The – Manor?" she asked.

"Things have proved more expensive than I anticipated," her uncle answered, "and to tell the truth I have had a bad run of luck at the tables."

"You have – lost money?" she asked almost in horror.

"Only a little. I have not risked much," her uncle replied, "but even a little is too much where you and I are concerned."

He walked across the room again before he went on,

"The whole situation is as difficult as I might have anticipated. Elaine cannot understand why I am cheeseparing where you are concerned and I dare not tell her the truth."

"She loves you, Uncle Roderick."

"I know that," her uncle retorted, "but there is nothing I can do about it."

For the first time Petula felt rather sorry for him. After all he was in the same position as she was, except that her situation was worse in that she had to think of the man she loved being married to somebody else.

She was certain that Mrs. Warren would never contemplate marriage with anyone except her uncle.

She showed by the expression in her eyes and the soft note in her voice how much she cared for him although she was very careful not to reveal it in any other way.

"I shall be disappointed," Sir Roderick was saying, "if you have to settle for Crowhurst. He is an excellent catch for someone like yourself. At the same time he is not in the same class as Temple Coombe."

"He is very – old, Uncle Roderick."

For the first time since they had been talking her uncle smiled.

"Then you will become a widow, my dear, when you are still comparatively young, with money to burn and every fortune-hunter in the country at your feet."

Petula looked at him in a startled manner.

"It is then," Sir Roderick went on, "that you will be able to be really kind to your poor uncle who has done his best for you."

The whole idea made Petula feel not only disgusted but degraded.

It was bad enough to have to marry a man for his money, but to plan what would happen after he was dead was, she told herself, horrible.

She also felt that her uncle was like a jailor incarcerating her in a golden prison that she could never escape from.

She thought how difficult it was going to be when she was married to keep on giving him money, apart from the fact that sooner or later her husband would have to know that she was not the heiress she had been acclaimed as being.

'I just cannot bear it,' she thought in despair.

She wanted to run away, to hide, to die if need be, rather than have to go on with this masquerade which seemed to become more menacing and more frightening day by day.

They went to balls, to Receptions, to Assemblies and Petula was also taken to Almack's which was the most formal and the most exclusive place to dance in the whole of the *Beau Monde*.

She was not invited to go to Carlton House or, if she was, her uncle refused for her. He went there himself occasionally, she gathered, although not as frequently as he pretended.

At the end of every evening she knew that if she was truthful she had once again been looking for one face.

One face only in the crowds that glittered, chattered, gossiped and seemed not only to look the same but to say the same things day after day and night after night.

Then, quite unexpectedly, when everything seemed miserable and dark with despair, she received a little basket of flowers.

It was very simple, very unpretentious and, when it was brought to her with several other floral arrangements that had been left at Berkeley Square, she hardly glanced at it.

Then she opened the card that was attached to the handle and the colour came into her pale face and she felt as if she had suddenly come alive.

The card contained only three words,

"From Major Wood."

Could any code be clearer to her and more mysterious to anyone else?

He was thinking of her as she had been thinking of him and the flowers when she looked at them told her everything she needed to know.

They were violets, white violets, and doubtless, as the Season for them was over, they had been difficult to find.

But she remembered the small white violets in the wood peeping beneath the leaves and knew that the Major had remembered them too.

Forgotten for the moment were her uncle's frightening plans, the old men she might have to marry and her terror of the future.

All she could think of was that the Duke still loved her as she loved him.

This evening they were to go to the Opera and afterwards have an early night because it being Saturday there was no great ball such as took place on other days of the week.

Mrs. Warren had an explanation for this.

"Mrs. Fitzherbert is a Roman Catholic," she said, "and does not approve of dancing on Sundays. It is not, of course, her opinion that matters directly, but then she has persuaded the Prince of Wales not to accept any invitations to balls given on Sundays."

"It will be nice to get to bed early for once," Petula replied.

"This is what I should be saying, not you at your age," Mrs. Warren laughed, "but I agree with you. However it will be a worry because I am sure that your uncle will gamble at one of his Clubs and it makes him so disagreeable if he loses."

Petula felt that he had every reason to be disagreeable, but she did not say so and they all three went and sat in a box at Covent Garden.

To Petula the Opera was delightful, but she was well aware that her uncle was bored.

Before the last act was half finished he hurried them away because he said it would be difficult to find their carriage when everyone left at the same time.

They arrived back at Berkeley Square and the old butler let them in, stifling a yawn as he did so.

"You need not stay up, Bruton," Sir Roderick said. "I will take the key with me as I may be very late."

"You are going to White's?" Mrs. Warren asked with a little cry.

Sir Roderick nodded.

"I promised to meet some of my friends," he told her evasively.

Petula was hardly listening.

There were two gifts of flowers standing on the table in the hall, one of them she realised at once came from Lord Crowhurst. She knew his handwriting by now and the other one was another small basket.

Quickly, in case her uncle should ask questions about it, she took the card from amongst the blooms and realised that it was enclosed in a sealed envelope.

As soon as her uncle had left, she then hurried up the stairs hardly waiting to kiss Mrs. Warren goodnight.

When she reached her room, she opened the envelope and found it contained just one line,

"*I am waiting for you in Curzon Street.*"

She stared at it feeling that she could hardly believe what she read, then with her heart beating tumultuously she ran to the wardrobe.

She took down a dark cloak that she had brought with her from the country, but which was far too dull and unfashionable to wear in London.

But it had a deep hood and she knew that it was important that she should not be seen or recognised at this time of the night.

She pulled the hood over her head, draped the cloak over the white gown she wore and tiptoed down the stairs.

As she expected, Bruton had hurried off to his own quarters. And at night Tomkins, the lady's maid who served both her and Mrs. Warren, concentrated on Mrs. Warren while Petula looked after herself.

In the hall there was only the one candle burning in a silver sconce. The rest had been economically extinguished.

It took her only a short second to open the door and slip outside.

Just for one moment she felt a little afraid as there was still a large number of people walking about and carriages with splendidly attired servants driving past.

Keeping to the shade of the houses she ran as swiftly as she dared towards Curzon Street.

The carriage was there, the door was open and she felt as though she flew into the inside of it like a bird seeking the security of its own nest.

Then the Duke's arms were around her and he was kissing her wildly, passionately and possessively.

She was breathless and at the insistence of his kisses she felt as if he awoke a fire within her to echo the fire on his lips and which she knew was smouldering in his eyes.

'I love you! I love you!' she wanted to shout out, but it was impossible to speak.

He held her so close that she knew that he had missed her as much as she had missed him.

The carriage drove away and once again stopped beside the Serpentine.

Now the water was not golden with sunshine but silver with the reflection of the stars.

"My precious, my life, my love!" the Duke said in an unsteady voice. "You are here – here in my arms after what has seemed a century of loneliness and agony without you."

"I-I have missed you – too," Petula stammered, "but I should not be here – only I had to come."

"And I had to see you. Oh, my darling, I have been so afraid that you would refuse and I should wait in vain."

"How did you know that we would be home early?" Petula asked him.

She thought he smiled as he laid his cheek against her hair.

"I know everything you have done this past ghastly week, but I dared not try to see you until I was alone."

Petula knew then that Lady Emelye had gone back to Yorkshire.

"Everyone is talking of your beauty and of your admirers," the Duke said. "It has driven me nearly insane!"

"I have had to – listen to – everyone talking about – you," Petula replied.

There was a little throb in her voice, which told the Duke how much it had hurt her.

"My darling, how can either of us bear it?" he cried despairingly.

Then he was kissing her again, kissing her with the desperation of a man who has seen everything he cares for slipping away from him.

"I love you!" he said at length. "I love you until it is impossible to think straight, but I know that we cannot go on like this."

"You mean – we must not – see each other?"

"I mean," he said slowly, "that we must be brave. We *have* to go away together."

He felt Petula stiffen and he then said,

"We will be married in France and not return to England until another scandal will prove more interesting than ours."

"B-but we cannot – we must not do that," Petula answered in a low voice.

"I know what you are thinking and I am thinking the same," the Duke answered. "But, my precious, just as you feel it impossible to marry another man, so I cannot marry anyone but you."

His arms tightened around her as he carried on,

"Even if you refuse to be my wife, I know that no other woman shall bear my name. It would be a sacrilege that I cannot contemplate and remain sane."

"But you are betrothed – you gave your – word," Petula murmured.

There was a little pause before the Duke replied to her,

"I have thought it all out very clearly. Tomorrow I am going to Yorkshire to tell Emelye and her parents the truth. And I intend to make them realise that I cannot and will not marry someone I do not love when my heart is elsewhere."

"They will be very – shocked."

"I am aware of that and they will also think it an insult, which might result in the Earl calling me out, but I think that is unlikely."

Petula gave a little cry.

"If he did, he might – kill you!"

"I am younger than he is and a far better shot," the Duke said. "But I assure you the Earl will be well aware that would cause an even greater scandal than the fact that I am refusing to marry his daughter."

He did not wait for Petula to answer, but went on,

"Naturally I will give Emelye the opportunity to jilt me before I state categorically that whether she does or does not I intend to marry you."

"How can I – let you do – this?" Petula asked in a very small voice.

At the same time something glorious and ecstatic was rising within her at the thought that he loved her so much that he would sacrifice his honour for her.

She knew it would be hard for him to go abroad for very long, to leave his estates, his horses and the Social position he held not only in London but in the country.

As if he knew what she was thinking, the Duke said,

"I must, of course, write to the King and ask him to relieve me of my duties at Court and in the County as his Lord Lieutenant."

"Am I – am I really – worth it?" Petula stuttered.

She turned her face up to his and, in the faint light from the moon and the glow of the lanterns, he could see the perfection of her features and her eyes looking up into his.

"For you," he sighed, "1 would go down into Hell and that is where I am every moment when you are not with me."

There was a depth of sincerity in his voice that made Petula quiver.

Then he said,

"I told you our love was different, my precious one, and that is exactly what it is. I love you, not only because you are just the most beautiful person I have ever seen in my life, but because my heart is your heart and we are a part of each other so that when you are not there I am no longer a whole man."

"When you – are not there," Petula replied, "I find I cannot – think. 1 cannot see or hear – what is happening around me."

"Then how can we let anything else matter?" the Duke asked simply. "Neither of us, my darling, can sentence ourselves to go through life maimed and crippled as we would be both mentally and spiritually without each other."

Petula made a little sound that was a sob but one of happiness.

She could hardly believe that this was happening. She could hardly realise that after so much suffering she could really be with the Duke and their dream of love could become one of reality.

"I love you! *I love – you*!" she whispered.

Then the Duke was kissing her once more until he evoked something wild and wonderful within her so that she kissed him back and clung to him until a raging fire seemed to consume them both.

*

"I worship you," the Duke said much later, "and now, my precious love, I must take you home."

"I cannot – leave you," Petula murmured.

"Soon we will be together every moment of the day and night," he said, "we will go to France, then to Italy. There are so many things I want to show you now that the War is over."

"I am – afraid that you will miss – " Petula began, but he interrupted her.

"I will miss nothing and nobody as long as I have you. All I want is to be with you, to love you and to teach you to love me."

"I do love you so much already."

"Not as much as I intend you will in the future," the Duke answered.

He kissed her forehead before he continued,

"You are so sweet, so pure and so innocent that I can imagine nothing more perfect or more absorbing than to teach you, my lovely one, about love."

"S-suppose after all you give up for me – I disappoint you?" Petula asked.

"I may disappoint you," he replied.

"You will never do that," she said quickly. "You are just so – magnificent and so – wonderful that there is not a man in the whole world like – you nor will there – ever be one!"

The Duke held her very close against him.

Then he said,

"Shall we walk for a moment under the trees and remind ourselves of the place where I first kissed you, when I knew exactly that you were what I had sought and never found and everything I really wanted in life?"

"Please – let us do – that."

The Duke opened the door and, before Jason could jump down from the box to hold it for them, he had helped Petula out.

It was cool and quiet under the trees and, when they were out of sight of the carriage, they stood beneath the branches with the silver water at their feet as the Duke put his arms around Petula.

He could see the loveliness of her face as she lifted it to his. He could feel the softness of her body as it melted against him and the passionate beating of her heart.

For a moment he did not kiss her, he only looked down at her.

Then he began,

"I pledge myself here and now to make you happy, to ensure that our love is greater and more tremendous than anything in the whole world or indeed in Heaven itself."

Petula drew in her breath and then she replied very softly,

"I will – try to make your sacrifice for me – worthwhile and I shall – live for you and love you with my – heart, my soul and my mind. I have – nothing else to – give you."

"Do you think I would want anything else?" he asked, then once again he was kissing her.

It seemed to Petula as if there was something sacred and Holy now in their kiss.

It was as if they had taken their vows at the Altar and had received the Blessing of God.

She felt as if he carried her up into the stars above them and that they were joined as one by the Divine Power that is life itself.

Then, with the Duke's arm round her, they walked back slowly and in silence towards the carriage, both feeling at peace and as if they had reached a harbour after passing through tumultuous and dangerous seas.

"So I shall leave for Yorkshire tomorrow," the Duke told her as the carriage drove off. "They are not expecting me until next week, but I dare not leave you alone for much longer because of what your uncle is planning for you."

"Nothing will – matter as long as you – come back to me," Petula sighed.

"Just play for time," the Duke advised. "You will understand, my darling, that I cannot talk to Sir Roderick until I have told Emelye what I intend to do."

"Will she be – very upset?"

The Duke seemed to consider this question for a moment.

"I do not think so. She is not in love with me as you and I are in love, but I think she is fond of me, after all we have known each other for so many years."

"It will be – difficult for you to – hurt her."

"I have no choice," the Duke answered. "Either I hurt her or you and myself."

"I do understand – as long as you will never – regret it afterwards."

"Never! Never! *Never*!" he almost swore and the last word was spoken against her lips.

The carriage stopped again at the corner of Curzon Street and, when Jason got down, the Duke said,

"Drive to the front door of 47 Berkeley Square."

"Very good, Your Grace."

Jason closed the door and, as Petula stared wide-eyed, the Duke said,

"I am through with pretence! I am through with hiding and sending you little anonymous baskets of flowers when really what I want to give you is the moon, the stars and the sun to express my love."

Petula understood what he was saying to her. Equally she hoped that her uncle by some unfortunate mischance was not returning at the same time that she was.

Then belatedly, because she was so bemused by what was happening, she said,

"I have just remembered – I cannot get in through the front door – After all you will have to take me to the Mews."

The Duke gave a short laugh.

"So much for my grandiose gesture. Never mind, when I return we will both of us use the front door together hand in hand."

Jason was told to go round to the Mews and the carriage took them there.

The place was in darkness, but the doors were open and Petula knew that her uncle had not returned.

The Duke kissed both of her hands and then her lips.

"I shall be away for six days, my darling," he said, "and then you can leave everything to me. I will look after you and you will never have to worry about anything again."

Petula laid her cheek against his hand as he held hers before the door of the carriage then opened and she stepped out.

She did not look back, but just hurried into the darkness of the stables along the passage that led to the house.

When she reached her room, she threw herself down on the bed trying to think and trying to realise what this would mean.

'I shall – belong to him, I shall be his – wife!' she told herself. 'Oh, God, how grateful I am!'

She lay for some time just as she was.

Then she pulled off her cloak and, without waiting to undress, knelt beside the bed to say a prayer of thanksgiving that God had blessed her in a way she had never imagined possible.

*

Petula awoke knowing that she had only slept for a few hours.

She had fallen asleep feeling that the Duke's arms were around her and his lips on hers.

She felt that the sunshine glinting through the sides of the curtains was more golden than it had ever been before.

The room seemed to be filled with the fragrance of flowers and the music that came from her own heart.

"Six days! Only six days!" she said aloud and knew that every minute that passed drew her closer to the moment when she would be with the Duke.

There was then a knock on the door and Tomkins came in.

She drew back the curtains before she piped up,

"I've called you much earlier than is usual, miss, as there's a note arrived for you a few minutes ago and the groom said 'twas of the utmost urgency and so should be given to you immediate-like!"

Petula sat up in bed and put out her hand eagerly to take the note.

There was no need to guess who it had come from and there was a look of radiance on her face that caused Tomkins to look at her curiously as she opened the envelope.

She saw that it contained two pages.

On one was written,

"My dearest most Beloved,
What else can I do?"

For a moment Petula felt she could not open the other piece of paper and when she did so she saw the engraved address at the top of it and felt as if it swam in front of her eyes.

It read,

"Kirkby Hall
Yorkshire.

My dear Adrian,
I am writing this and sending it post-haste to London to ask you to come here with all possible speed. Emelye went riding this morning immediately after her arrival and had a very bad fall.

The doctors think she may have broken her back which means she may be paralysed. She is asking for you and I can only beg of you to reach us without a moment's delay. I have sent to Windsor for her mother.

All it remains to say is that I am just heartbroken at what has happened, an accident which is quite inexplicable.

Yours,
Kirkby.

Petula read it through twice and on the second time she felt as though the letter itself was covered in darkness.

She had thanked God too prematurely. She had grasped at her happiness and now it had eluded her.

From a long way away she heard Tomkins say,

"You look as though you've had a bad shock, miss. Is there anythin' I can do for you?"

"No – nothing," Petula answered.

That was the right answer. There was nothing anyone could do!

Without really being conscious of her movements, Petula dressed and only as she walked downstairs did she realise that it was only a little after six-thirty.

Vaguely at the back of her mind she thought of writing a letter to the Duke and then she knew there was no point in it and anyway he would have already left for Yorkshire.

She went into the library hardly seeing any of her surroundings, conscious only of a pain that seemed to grow and grow in its intensity until it filled not only her whole being but the world and there was nothing but agony.

Then so suddenly that it made her start the door was opened and her uncle stood there.

She looked at him and thought for a moment that he must have had an accident.

There was an expression that she did not understand on his face, his white cravat was a limp rag round his throat and he held in both hands his high crowned hat.

"Petula," he said in a voice that was so hoarse it was little more than just a croak, "I am brilliant! I am a genius! You see before you a man who possesses a fortune!"

Petula stared at him incredulously, then slowly he tipped up his hat and a shower of gold coins, notes of hand and cheques fell from it to the floor.

"Twenty thousand pounds at least! A fortune!" Sir Roderick cried. "A *fortune*, Petula!"

He swayed as he stood there and Petula ran to his side to take his arm.

"You are ill, Uncle Roderick."

"Not ill – *drunk*!" he replied. "Drunk with joy and the thought that never again need I touch a damned card."

She helped him to a chair and he sprawled in it, his legs outstretched.

"A fortune," he repeated beneath his breath, his words slightly slurred. "I am a very rich man!"

Petula stood looking at him for a few moments, then at the carpet bestrewn with money. Turning, she ran up the stairs to Mrs. Warren's room.

She entered the room without knocking and hurried across it to draw back the curtains.

As the sunshine came flooding in, she turned round to see Mrs Warren sitting up in bed staring at her with startled eyes.

"It is Uncle Roderick," Petula replied breathlessly. "He needs you! Come downstairs to him."

"There has not been an accident?" Mrs. Warren cried.

Even as she spoke she began to climb out of bed.

"There has been no accident, but he will tell you what has happened," Petula answered.

Mrs. Warren was looking attractive in a lace-trimmed muslin cap that she always wore over her hair at night.

Petula picked up her robe, also trimmed with lace, which lay over a chair and helped her into it.

"Hurry!" she suggested. "He is in the library and will want to tell you himself what has occurred."

"I do hope it is nothing disastrous," Mrs. Warren murmured in an anxious voice.

Then spurred by Petula's air of urgency she slipped her feet into her soft slippers and still buttoning her robe began to walk down the corridor towards the stairs.

Sir Roderick was lying prone in the chair where Petula had left him, but now his eyes were closed and she knew that he had fallen asleep from drink and exhaustion.

Mrs. Warren stepped over the money without really noticing it and went to Sir Roderick to kneel down beside him.

"Roderick!" she called. "Roderick!"

It seemed as if her voice awoke him, but he only opened his eyes to say once again in an incoherent voice,

"I am a rich – man!"

"He has been gambling all night," Petula explained to her. "He has only arrived home a few minutes ago."

Mrs. Warren then looked for the first time at the money scattered over the carpet.

"He has – won all that?" she asked in an incredulous tone.

"So he told me," Petula replied.

Mrs. Warren rose a little uncertainly to her feet.

"Is it – possible?" she whispered.

"It is not only possible but it means, dearest Mrs. Warren, that now you can be married and you can look after him."

She put her arms round the older woman and kissed her, thinking as she did so that no one would ever say the same words to her.

She felt the tears come into her eyes and said hastily,

"Will you look after Uncle Roderick?"

Without waiting for an answer she went from the room closing the door behind her.

She ran upstairs and rang the bell.

When Tomkins appeared, she said to her,

"Will you please pack my trunk up for me? I cannot take everything, but perhaps the rest can follow later."

"You are goin' away, miss?"

"Yes," Petula answered resolutely, "I am going away."

As Tomkins began packing, she changed into a gown she thought suitable for travelling.

Then she took down from the wardrobe the dark cloak she had worn when she had gone with the Duke into the Park at night.

It brought back memories that she hastily pushed to one side to choose the plainest of her bonnets, knowing that most of them would attract a great deal of comment and speculation amongst the travellers in a stagecoach.

"We'll have to get another trunk, miss," Tomkins pointed out.

"This trunk will be enough for now," Petula replied. "My evening gowns and bonnets can stay here. I will not need them."

"Not need them?" Tomkins repeated in some surprise, but Petula did not enlighten her as to why they would be unnecessary.

Instead, picking up her gloves and a handbag, she went down the stairs, spoke to Bruton who was in the hall and then went into the library.

Her uncle was still fast asleep, but then Mrs. Warren was sitting at the desk counting the money she had collected from the floor.

She looked up as Petula entered and said in an awestruck voice,

"Twenty-one thousand, five hundred pounds. I cannot believe it!"

"Uncle Roderick said he would never touch a card again and that is a promise you must make him keep."

A faint smile touched Mrs. Warren's lips.

"He never really enjoyed gambling."

Petula looked at the piles of gold guineas in front of her and asked,

"Will you give me one hundred pounds and tell Uncle Roderick when he wakes up that I asked for it?"

Mrs. Warren looked at her with a question in her eyes and Petula explained,

"I am going away. Uncle Roderick will explain it to you that I am not the heiress that I pretended to be, but now I am – free!"

"My dearest child – " Mrs. Warren expostulated, but Petula held up her hand.

"I would rather Uncle Roderick told you everything," she said, "and, as I want to avoid arguments and since I am certain that he would much prefer to be alone with you, I want to leave before he wakes up."

"Then take anything you want," Mrs. Warren suggested with a little gesture of her hand towards the piles of money.

Petula selected eight ten pound notes and picked up ten guineas, which she required for her journey. She put it all in her handbag and then said,

"If we never meet again, I really want to thank you for all your kindness to me and for introducing me so cleverly to the Social world."

She kissed Mrs. Warren as she spoke, but did not wait to answer the questions that she saw hovering on her lips.

She merely walked out of the room closing the door behind her.

Her trunk was already in the hall and Bruton had on her instructions called for a Hackney carriage.

He and the coachman lifted the trunk onto the front of it and Petula climbed in behind.

"Goodbye, Bruton," she said to the butler. "I think Sir Roderick and Mrs. Warren would like you to take some black coffee to the library."

"Very good, miss," the butler answered, "and I hopes you has a good journey."

"Thank you," Petula answered him. "Will you instruct the coachman to go to *The Two-Necked Swan* in Islington?"

Bruton shouted the words out to the coachman who appeared to be rather deaf. Then he whipped up his tired horse and they started to move through Berkeley Square.

Petula remembered how the Duke had proposed to drive to the front door of Number 47 saying,

"*I am through with pretence. I am through with hiding!*"

He had spoken too quickly, she thought, and it was perhaps prophetic that, after what he had called his 'grandiose gesture', he had had after all to take her round to the back of the Mews.

She remembered how he had laughed and said,

"*When I return, we will both use the front door together, hand in hand.*"

Now that would never happen!

He would be tied to Emelye not only legally but morally in such a way that Petula knew would preclude them even from seeing each other secretly.

Could they feel anything but guilt if they had deceived a woman who was paralysed and could therefore not compete for his affections?

This was the end.

By a twist and turn of Fate that at the very last moment her happiness had been snatched away from her, leaving only the utter darkness of despair without even a single ray of hope.

CHAPTER SEVEN

It took Petula very nearly five days to reach Buckden and the journey was excessively uncomfortable in hot crowded stagecoaches.

Passengers received little or no attention at the Posting inns they had stopped at and so only the cheapest and most uncomfortable rooms were offered them where they stayed each night.

Eventually she reached the nearest hamlet on the highway to Buckden and there she had to wait for a carrier to convey her the last four miles to the village.

When she drove down the dusty lane and then had her first sight of the little Greystone Church where her father and mother were buried in the churchyard, she knew that nothing had changed since she had gone away, but for her life would never be the same.

It was as if she had been shipwrecked and in the traumatic experience had lost so much of her original self that she was now a different person altogether.

The carrier, whom she knew well because he had been coming to the village ever since her childhood, drew up outside Honeysuckle Cottage and Petula saw that since she had seen it last the garden had been tidied and was bright with flowers.

She opened the latch gate and walked down the small path bordered by pinks.

Even as she reached the door, it opened and Annie stood there smiling.

"Miss Petula!" she exclaimed. "I couldn't believe my very eyes when I saw you through the window."

"I have come home, Annie," Petula told her with a little break in her voice.

The carrier carried in her trunk and she pulled off her bonnet and looked round the small sitting room.

It was filled with all the special pieces of furniture and little treasures that her mother had accumulated and loved.

There were ornaments of little or no intrinsic value, but to Petula they were part of her childhood and part too, she thought, of the future that remained for her.

She paid the carrier and he thanked her for a generous tip and touched his forelock.

"You gave him too much, Miss Petula," Annie said in the scolding voice that she knew so well. "Have you come into a fortune all of a sudden?"

"All the money we have in the world is in this bag," Petula answered as she set it down on the table. "It will have to last us, Annie, for a long time."

She spoke in such a strange voice that instantly Annie went to her.

"What's the matter? What's happened to you, dearie?" she enquired anxiously.

There was so much solicitude and the gentleness she had known as a child in Annie's words that Petula burst into tears.

*

The Duke, driving towards Yorkshire felt a despair that he knew Petula as well must be feeling.

The letter had come out of the blue and he knew at once that it destroyed all his plans of happiness for the future in a way that nothing else could have done.

If Emelye was paralysed from a fall out riding, and he knew exactly what that meant, it would be impossible for him to refuse to marry her.

Doubtless out of consideration she would offer to release him from his promise, but only an outsider, a man with no principles whatsoever, would throw over the woman to whom he was engaged to be married because she was suddenly incapacitated.

It might have put paid to his happiness, it might mean that he could never have an heir to succeed him. But the code by which a gentleman lived and was recognised laid down that his behaviour in such circumstances must be chivalrous and beyond reproach.

Only by driving at a speed which required every ounce of his concentration did the Duke prevent himself from crying out aloud at his own despair and unhappiness.

The Countess of Kirkby had been commanded to stay at Windsor in attendance on the Queen and, as she was an hereditary Lady of the Bedchamber, it was impossible for her to refuse.

The Earl and Emelye had left for Yorkshire together and the Duke had been aware that Emelye was longing to go back to her horses.

"I have two in training which are going to be really superlative," she said to him. "I told Edward Trafford to raise the jumps while I was away, after which I am quite certain that they will be capable of going round any classic Steeplechase course with the greatest of ease."

The Duke knew that Edward Trafford was her father's Steeplechase trainer and had a big reputation in the racing world.

He had, however, said to her,

"Be careful, Emelye. Those sort of jumps are hard enough for a man let alone a woman."

"You might say that to most women," Emelye replied, "but not to me."

The Duke had smiled.

"No. You are certainly exceptional. At the same time very high jumps can be dangerous, as we both know."

He was thinking that one of the Earl's horses had broken a leg the previous year in one of the classic Steeplechases and had to be destroyed.

As if she deliberately put his warning out of her mind, Emelye had gone on to talk of the horses she was training.

There were some foals that had been born to a very expensive thoroughbred mare which the Earl had purchased three years ago.

"You will have to improve your stable, Adrian," she said teasingly, "and, of course, once we are married I will help you."

"Thank you," the Duke had replied rather sarcastically.

His horses had won more races and so were considered on the whole to be of far better stock than the Earl's.

As the Duke expected to be travelling to Yorkshire fairly frequently, he had already sent his horses to every important Posting inn and he therefore reached Kirkby Castle in record time.

As he drew his sweating team to a standstill, the Earl came hurrying down the steps from the front door saying,

"I did not expect you so soon, Adrian, but it is good of you to arrive so quickly."

"How is Emelye?" the Duke asked him.

He was hot and rather tired and would have very much liked to bathe, but he knew there was no chance of that.

"I promised to take you to her right away," the Earl answered. "She has asked for no one else ever since the accident."

"What happened?" the Duke asked as they started to climb the staircase.

"She insisted on having a jump raised even higher than Trafford advised. Even so it was a mystery how she managed to fall in the way she did. The stallion hardly grazed his knees."

The Duke did not reply and they walked along the corridor in silence.

The Earl knocked very softly on a door and it was opened by the Countess looking very drawn and lined.

She held out both her hands.

"Adrian. Thank God you are here! I only arrived this morning to find Emelye asking for you and she will not rest until she has seen you."

"How is she?" the Duke asked her automatically.

The Countess's lips moved silently and the tears came into her eyes so that there was no need for words.

The Duke walked past her into the dimly lit room and moved towards the bed. Emelye was lying very still in the centre of it and her eyes were closed.

"Emelye," he called in a low voice.

Her eyes opened slowly and he felt that they focused on him with some difficulty. And then there was a faint smile on her lips.

The Duke took her hand in his.

"I am sorry."

"Are – we – alone?"

She had some difficulty in saying the words and, although they were low, he could hear her clearly.

He glanced towards the door that the Countess had closed behind him.

"Quite alone."

"Then – listen Adrian. I have – something to – ask of you."

"You know I will do anything you want."

"I am – going to – die."

"No, of course not – " he began.

"Don't – argue with me," she said, "just – listen. I have – not long."

The Duke held her hand and waited.

"I want you – to give Edward enough – money to go to – America. He must – get away – but he – cannot afford – to go unless you help him."

"Edward Trafford?" the Duke questioned her bewildered.

"Yes, Edward – " Emelye said. "He – cannot stay here."

"What are you saying to me?" the Duke asked.

"I – meant to – fall," Emelye said. "It was not – the horse's fault. I meant – to kill – myself."

"But why, Emelye? *Why?*" the Duke insisted.

"I am having – Edward's baby. The Doctor has – promised not to – tell Papa and Mama until I am – dead. Then – he says he – must do so."

The Duke was silent from sheer surprise as Emelye went on in a slightly weaker voice,

"There is no one – I can ask but – you. Promise me – you will help Edward – I have loved him – ever since I was a – child when he – first taught me to ride."

Her voice almost faded away on the last words and the Duke said,

"I promise you. I will give him the money to leave the country."

"And – enough to start – again in America?"

"All he needs," the Duke answered.

Emelye gave a sigh.

"Thank you – Adrian. I know – I have been – a fool – but it was – worth it. We were – so happy until – Papa informed me that I had to – marry you."

The Duke lifted her hand to his lips.

Then she said,

"Tell – Edward they will not – let me see him, but you tell him – I am not – afraid to die – and I love him!"

"I will tell him."

Emelye then closed her eyes and he felt that, as if now she had accomplished what she wanted, she was drifting away deliberately letting go of life.

"Emelye," the Duke called insistently. "*Emelye!*"

But her hand became limp in his and, although she was still breathing, he knew without being told that she would not live long.

He rose from the bed and went to the door to call her father and mother into the room.

*

Petula, tidying away the cups and saucers after she and Annie had finished their tea, then carried them into the small kitchen and put them down in the sink.

Everything was exceedingly neat and tidy and the cottage itself made her feel as if she was living in a dolls' house.

It seemed so minute after Berkeley Square and the rambling dilapidated old Manor. And, because Annie had squeezed so many things into the small rooms, Petula felt that sometimes she was as large as a giantess in a Lilliputian land.

She found in the cottage not only the things she had given Annie but that a large number of other bits and pieces from The Manor were there as well.

"Mr. Barrowick throws them out, if you can believe it," Annie related. "He told Adam, whom he's taken into his employment with a lot of others from the village, to burn them. Did you ever hear of such vandalism?"

Petula found it hard not to laugh at the indignation in Annie's voice, but when she went upstairs she did in fact laugh even though the traces of tears were still on her cheeks.

One of the things that Mr. Barrowick had not considered good enough for himself was the big four-poster bed her father had always slept in as had generations of Buckdens.

Annie had placed it in the largest of the bedrooms and it had left practically no room for anything else.

"Oh, Annie, how could you have that here?" Petula exclaimed.

"It was the Master's bed and it wasn't right that anyone else should have it," Annie said stoutly.

"How on earth did you get it up the stairs?"

"Adam carved it into pieces, then he and Ned put them together again."

They had made a good job of it Petula had to admit.

At the same time it seemed ridiculous that the best and largest bedroom in Honeysuckle Cottage should be filled with a carved four-poster with ancient red curtains emblazoned with the Buckden Coat of Arms.

Although it was faded and frayed it still seemed, Petula thought, to have a pride about it, which she told herself that she must try to emulate.

Annie had, of course, insisted that she should sleep in her father's bed and inevitably the person she thought of in the long dark hours of the night was the man who had used it last.

She would lie there pretending that the Duke's arms were round her and his lips were on hers.

Then, because she yearned and ached for him, she would find herself crying helplessly and miserably until from sheer exhaustion she fell asleep.

As she dried the saucers and put them on the shelf, Annie said,

"I'm just goin' to slip out and get somethin' for dinner. Is there anythin' you'd fancy, dearie?"

"I-I am not – hungry."

"You'll eat even if I have to stand over you and make you do it," Annie snapped. "It's so thin you're gettin'. I'll be askin' the new Doctor one of these days to come and see what be wrong with you."

"There is nothing – wrong with me," Petula replied. "I am just – not hungry."

Annie's lips tightened, which meant, Petula knew, that she would spend more money than was necessary in trying to tempt her with good food.

She knew there was no use arguing with Annie even while she resented the money Annie would insist on spending and knowing that even a hundred pounds would not last for ever.

She had not heard from her uncle since she had left London and she wondered if he was angry at her leaving. However she felt he would know by now that he had plenty of money himself and be relieved.

If she was to be truthful, she was not worrying about a letter from her uncle, but hoping against hope that there would be one from the Duke.

'If he does write to me, it will be to London,' she told herself. 'But there is nothing either of us can say to the other, so why do I go on longing to hear from him?'

She heard the cottage door close behind Annie and she suddenly wanted to go to the little wood.

The idea had been in her mind ever since she returned to Buckden, but she had known that it would be agonising to recapture the magic of that first kiss that she had forced herself to stay in the cottage.

She had learnt from both Annie and Adam that The Manor itself was a hive of activity.

Mr. Barrowick had brought in an army of builders, carpenters and stonemasons to restore the house to its original glory.

"He fancies he's the Prince of Wales and so is a-spendin' money like water," Annie said scornfully.

Petula had already learnt that most of the people from the village thought it extremely presumptuous that Mr. Barrowick should try to take the place of her father.

She knew, as it was getting late in the afternoon, that the workmen who had come some distance to the village would have gone home and it would therefore be safe for her to walk without being seen across the lawn and down the field to the little wood.

Without bothering to put on her bonnet because there was a path winding at the back of the village and into the shrubberies, Petula found her way and saw that the gardens that had grown so wild were already being trimmed into shape.

The lawns had been cut and she had learnt from Adam that they were to be extended right down to the edge of the wood itself.

The field was still a little rough, but Petula thought only of reaching the shadow of the birch trees. Yet, when she reached them, they seemed to swim before her eyes.

The violets had gone and so had the primroses and the bluebells. The leaves were thicker on the trees, but still the sun percolated golden through them to make a pattern on the ground beneath them.

Now it was the evening sun, lacking the pale shining gold of the morning sun that had shone so brilliantly when she had seen the Major coming towards her between the trunks of the trees.

She stood for a moment feeling the sensations and emotions she had known next sweep over her like a tidal wave.

Then there had been the magical enchantment, but now it had deepened and intensified until her whole being throbbed not only at the memory of it but because it was lost.

'Oh, God, help me to – forget,' she prayed suddenly.

Then her tears blinded her so that she could no longer see the sunshine.

*

The funeral was over and the Duke knew that now there was nothing to keep him at The Castle.

Emelye had been laid to rest in a churchyard at the end of the Park and, because the Earl and Countess were so heart-broken, it had been a very quiet Ceremony with only a few close friends and relations and those who worked on the estate present.

Before it took place the Duke had, however, been very busy.

He had not only given Edward Trafford the money he had promised Emelye he would, but he had also arranged for his passage to America and given him introductions to various owners and breeders when he arrived there.

"I don't know why you should do all this for me, my Lord," Trafford had said.

"I do not intend to discuss it with you," the Duke answered. "All I am concerned with is keeping any knowledge of it from the Earl and Countess."

He spoke so coldly as he considered Trafford, who was a much older man, had behaved extremely reprehensibly towards a young girl while he was in the Earl's employment.

He told himself that he had at the moment no wish to censure anyone, but only to make everything pass off as smoothly as Emelye would have wished.

He had had a difficult time with the Doctor who considered it his duty to inform the Earl and Countess of the real reason for their daughter's death.

The Duke had used all his persuasive powers.

The real difficulty lay in the fact that the Doctor was a good straightforward man who was extremely shocked at what had occurred.

Finally after nearly one hour's argument the Doctor had capitulated and given the Duke his word of honour that he would never divulge to anyone Emelye's condition when she died.

Now the Duke knew that his part in the proceedings was over and he would no longer have to pretend, which had been exceedingly difficult, that he himself was very upset.

The Earl came into the room and the Duke suggested,

"I think now that you and your wife would wish to be alone. So I have given orders for my things to be packed and my phaeton to be brought round to the door."

"You are leaving us?" the Earl exclaimed.

The Duke nodded and with some difficulty restrained the Earl from making a speech of gratitude and managed to leave without his saying 'goodbye' to the Countess who he guessed after the funeral would be weeping in her bedroom.

As he drove away down the drive with Jason beside him, he felt as if a burden had fallen from his shoulders and for the first time he was free to think about himself.

"The travellin' landau's gone ahead of us, Your Grace," Jason said. "They asked where you'd be stayin' tonight and I says as I thought it would be at that inn near Huntingford."

"Yes, it will certainly do," he replied absent-mindedly, "though we need not change horses there."

"No, Your Grace. When we stops for luncheon tomorrow will be soon enough."

Suddenly the Duke remembered that Huntingford was not far from Buckden and it was the inn that Petula had referred to when he had asked where he could stay.

He had a sudden feeling that he must go to Buckden, to look at the place where he had first met her.

Yet some undefinable instinct within him made him feel that he should go there not only to reminisce, but for some other reason.

He told himself that now the evenings were light until eleven o'clock or later he would have plenty of time to visit Buckden and then reach Huntingford before it was dark.

While the Duke preferred to travel in his phaeton, his valet and any other servants who were necessary then went ahead of him in a travelling landau carrying besides themselves a multitudinous pile of luggage.

It ensured his comfort in that when he arrived at an inn everything he needed had been unpacked, the bed had been remade with his own linen, his dinner had been ordered and the wine he was likely to prefer brought up from the cellars.

He accepted such luxuries automatically now that he had inherited the Dukedom, but, because he had been a soldier he was, as he had told Petula, ready when it was necessary to rough it.

There was, however, no need now for that and tonight, even if he wished to do so, he would not be able to sleep in the dilapidated Manor as it no longer belonged to the Buckdens.

He could understand Petula resenting, although they had never had time to talk about it, her uncle selling the house and the estate which had been in their family for so many years.

But he told himself that once they were married she would have very many magnificent houses in which to be the Chatelaine that she would never regret losing her old home.

At the same time he wanted to go to Buckden.

'I am being sentimental,' he told himself, and knew that it was a mild way to express his feelings where Petula was concerned.

Jason was surprised when they turned off the main road at five o'clock and started down the twisting lane that led to the village where he had had the accident.

"We be goin' to Buckden, Your Grace?" the groom asked after a moment.

"Yes," the Duke replied.

He volunteered no further information and they drove on in silence until the small grey Church with its pointed spire came into sight.

Then, as the Duke drove his team more slowly, Jason gave an exclamation,

"There's the Nanny to Miss Petula, Your Grace," he said, "who looked after us when we stayed at The Manor that night."

The Duke looked where he pointed.

There was no mistaking Annie in her neat black bonnet and, despite the heat, wearing a grey woollen shawl over her grey gown.

The Duke drew the phaeton to a standstill beside her and she stared at him in surprise.

"Why it be Major Chester!" she exclaimed. "Fancy seein' you again, sir."

"I have not forgotten how kind and hospitable you were when we came to The Manor," the Duke replied.

"I can't be offerin' hospitality there anymore, sir," Annie answered. "It's been sold and I'm livin' here now in Honeysuckle Cottage."

The Duke saw that he had drawn up his horses almost opposite a small thatched cottage standing by itself and with its porch covered in honeysuckle.

"It certainly looks very attractive and worthy of its name," the Duke remarked.

"It's small but comfortable," Annie answered.

She hesitated and then added,

"If you'd be likin' a little refreshment, sir, I'm sure Miss Petula would be pleased to see you."

The Duke started so that for a moment his hand on the reins tightened.

Then he asked,

"Is Miss Petula here?"

"Yes, sir. She came back from London some days ago and judgin' by her appearance it did her no good."

The Duke handed the reins to Jason.

"I shall be very glad to avail myself of your offer," he said to Annie and got down from the phaeton.

*

Petula fought against giving way to her tears.

What was the point, she asked herself, of crying when she should really be grateful for having known a happiness which she was sure was accorded to very few people.

She was ashamed for having wept so bitterly every night, yet it was impossible to deny the yearning of her whole body for the man she loved and who she knew loved her.

Perhaps, she thought, it would have been better if he did not care rather than to know that this terrible gulf between them existed, a gulf that it was impossible to bridge.

'I must be brave,' she said, 'and I will not come here again.'

She must have been in the wood for a long time and she thought that she would take one last look at the beauty of her surroundings.

Then it would be etched for ever in her mind and she would remember it only when she was brave enough to think of the love and the wonder that she had found there.

She pulled out her handkerchief and wiping her eyes almost fiercely she started to retrace her steps back to Annie and the cottage.

Suddenly she thought that she must be dreaming.

Someone was coming towards her through the panoply of trees and she imagined for one wild moment that she had stepped back in time and was seeing what had happened before and seeing it so clearly and so vividly that he was almost real.

Then, as the Duke came nearer, she knew that he was real!

For a moment she could only stand looking at him as if she had been turned to stone and then with a little cry which seemed to echo amongst the trees she ran towards him.

She then flung herself against him and as his arms went round her it was impossible even to ask why he was here or what was happening.

His lips came down on hers and she could think of nothing but the wonder of his kiss and the rapture that swept through her like a shaft of sunlight.

He was with her now, she was close to him and he was drawing her heart, as he had done before, from between her lips and then she was his. His completely and absolutely and it was impossible to think of anything else.

The Duke held her closer and still closer and somewhere in the depths of her soul Petula prayed that she might die because she had never known such happiness and perhaps it would never come again.

At last the Duke raised his head and looked down at her.

At her mouth, soft from his kisses, at her eyes misty with tears looking up into his, at her cheeks pale from the intensity of the feelings that made her whole body tremble against his.

"My precious! My darling!" he said. "I have found you again and everything is all right."

He saw her eyes widen and he went on,

"We can be together and now nothing in the whole world can prevent it."

Petula gave a little cry of sheer happiness and then the Duke was kissing her again.

He kissed her until the wood swam dizzily around her and she felt as if the sunshine was so blinding that she could no longer see.

But it became a part of them both so that they glowed with a spiritual light.

"I love you! Oh, Adrian – I love – you so much!" she whispered, "and I thought I should never see you – again."

"Not only will you see me, but you will be with me always and for ever, my darling," the Duke said. "We are to be married this evening so we had better go to the cottage now."

"M-married?"

Petula could hardly breathe the word.

"I have spoken to the Vicar who told me that he has known you since you were a baby. I have explained to him because I am in mourning that our marriage has to be very quiet and a secret and he has agreed that no one shall know of it except for your Nanny."

"Oh – Adrian!"

Petula could hardly speak or breathe.

"You will understand the need for so much secrecy when I tell you that Emelye is dead."

Petula was still.

"The fall – killed her?"

"Yes, it killed her."

"It must have been very – upsetting for you."

"She told me before she died that she loved somebody else," he said. "That knowledge, my precious one, as you will understand, sets me free, free from the prickings of conscience or any feeling of guilt."

He had told himself as he drove away from Kirkby Castle that was all the story Petula need ever know.

Now he felt her give a deep sigh as if she also felt free and absolved from any qualms of disloyalty.

"We are – really to be – married?" she asked him again.

The Duke's arms tightened around her.

"Do you really think I could risk waiting any longer to make you mine before something else prevents you from becoming my wife?"

"How – did you know I was – here?"

"I must have felt it in my bones," the Duke answered, "and so I might ask you the same question."

Petula smiled.

"The morning after I received your letter," she said, 'Uncle Roderick came back from the Club having won over twenty thousand pounds."

"So you came home, my precious."

She had known that he would understand and she said simply,

"There was no reason for me to stay."

"No, of course not," the Duke answered, "and I am so grateful, darling, that my instinct where you are concerned has saved me many days of driving. I was on my way to London to find you."

"Perhaps it was Fate that brought us together again, as it did in the first place," Petula sighed.

"If it was Fate, then it has given us some uncomfortable moments," the Duke said dryly. "But now all its twist and turns with our love are over and, once you become my wife, I am prepared to defy the Heavens themselves to keep us apart."

He kissed her again, then with his arm round her they walked back towards Honeysuckle Cottage.

*

The sun had sunk down and in the dusky sky the first stars were appearing as Petula and the Duke moved into the tiny sitting room of the cottage.

It was so small and low-ceilinged that it made the Duke look almost abnormally tall and yet so attractive and elegant that Petula instinctively moved towards him, knowing from the expression in his eyes that he was waiting for her to do so.

After they had been married in the small Church, with only Annie present weeping tears of happiness into her handkerchief, they had come back to eat a delicious meal.

It made them both remember the first dinner she and Annie had given 'the Major' when the only food available had been a rabbit snared by Adam.

Tonight Annie had excelled herself with what she had already bought from the butcher to tempt Petula and the extras that she sent Jason to procure for her.

As the Duke put his arms round Petula, he said,

"I cannot help feeling amused, my darling, when I have some very magnificent houses waiting for my wife and my Duchess that we should start our married life in a cottage."

"Do you – mind?" Petula enquired a little anxiously.

"Mind?" he replied. "It does not matter where I am as long as I am with you. And I think we shall always feel that Honeysuckle Cottage was a uniquely romantic place for us to begin our honeymoon in."

"I was thinking in the wood before you came," Petula said, "that your wonderful kisses would be all I should have to – remember in the future."

But now it was impossible to find words for what she felt and, as if the Duke understood, he kissed her very gently before he said,

"Buckden will have a very special place in our hearts, my darling, and perhaps we will come back here to revive the ecstasy we both felt when I first kissed you and when 1 knew today that I should never lose you."

He paused.

"And there will be another memory more precious than either of those."

His lips were on her hair as he said very softly,

"It is right here, here in Buckden in Honeysuckle Cottage where I will make you mine completely and absolutely, now and for all time.'

"I did not know it was – possible to be so – happy," Petula whispered.

"That is what I will do," he promised, "and, my darling, I am very impatient to show you how much I love you."

Petula hid her face against his chest.

He held her close for a moment and then he put his fingers under her chin to look at her.

"You are just so beautiful, so breathtakingly beautiful," he said, "but my love for you is much more than that. As I have told you before and shall tell you again you are a part of me and I cannot possibly live without you."

He drew her close again as he went on,

"You are mine, Petula, mine not only for our whole lifetime together but for Eternity and far beyond. I believe that when a man and a woman are inseparably one then, where love is concerned, there is no such thing as death."

"I thought when we were being married that God had – brought us – together," Petula said breathlessly, "and nothing – nothing in the whole Universe could ever divide us."

She lifted her lips to the Duke's and he kissed her as if she was infinitely precious.

"I have not told you that Annie has – my father's – bed here," Petula said. "It was – where you – slept when you stayed at The Manor and every night – I have thought of you and – pretended that I was – in your arms."

"Tonight there will be no pretence," the Duke replied, "but must I wait much longer? I am tired of waiting for you, Petula, and of being afraid of losing you and your enchantment."

There was a note of passion in his voice that made Petula feel wildly excited and yet at the same time very shy.

He felt her quiver next to him as he said very softly,

"I want you! I want you, my darling one. It is now almost night, a night that will never be long enough for me."

Petula heard the yearning in his words and, as she raised her face to him, she whispered,

"I – want you too! Will you – come with – me?"

She knew that this was what the Duke wanted to hear, knew it by the sudden tightening of his arms, by the beating of his heart and by the fire she could see in his eyes.

Then with his arms round her and his lips on hers he drew her towards the door and up the twisting narrow staircase.

It led them into the small room that was filled with the great four-poster bed, which had served the Buckdens faithfully for so many generations.

Overhead the stars came out one by one and there was only the shrill squeak of bats and two voices murmuring over and over again,

"I love – you! *I love – you!*"

Manufactured by Amazon.ca
Acheson, AB